THREE GRAVES TO FARGO

Somewhere in the middle of Dakota Territory was a fortune in hidden gold, the proceeds of the Beanville gold heist, and now two men are headed north to stake their claim. It was not going to be a picnic though. It meant journeying into a bleak country, and to add to the dangers there was still a handful of persistent and vigilant lawmen who had refused to close the file on the long-lost fortune. Not for the first time the combination of gold and greed would bring grim death to many. Would Gentry, who had lost everything, finally survive?

THREE GRAVES TO FARGO

THREE GRAVES TO FARGO

by

Ethan Wall

Dales Large Print Books
Long Preston, North Yorkshire,
BD23 4ND, England.

British Library Cataloguing in Publication Data.

Wall, Ethan
Three graves to Fargo.

A catalogue record of this book is available from the British Library

ISBN 1-84262-406-7 pbk

First published in Great Britain 2004 by Robert Hale Limited

Published in Large Print 2005 by arrangement with Robert Hale Ltd.

Dales Large Print is an imprint of Library Magna Books Ltd.

Printed and bound in Great Britain by
T.J. (International) Ltd., Cornwall, PL28 8RW

For Craig T
(with thanks for putting up
with me over the years)

ONE

The night was reaching out across the sandy wastes and placing its dark hand on the town as a lone rider entered the main street. He rode the length of the main drag to fetch up at the picket fence that marked the graveyard. Above and beyond, faint light flickered at the stained-glass windows of the church. He dismounted, tethered his horse to the fence and moved up to the building along the path between the wooden crosses and assorted markers.

Inside he took off his hat. He stood peering through the gloom, the only light coming from half a dozen big candles spaced around the casket before the altar at the far end. He heard a cough and turned to see an old woman sitting on a chair, keeping vigil near the door.

He nodded to her and walked up the aisle. He moved to the foot of the casket and considered the laid-out figure. The delicate satin draped over the hands and lower parts looked incongruous against the dusty range-gear of the corpse.

He looked at the face of the dead man. 'So it *is* you,' he whispered. 'At long last.' Quietly he chuckled to himself in satisfaction, and added, '*Adios*, you son of a bitch.'

'Yeah,' the corpse said, '*Adios*, you son of a bitch.' Up came a hand, bearing a heavy .44. The weapon exploded twice, sending the visitor careering back to end up against polished wooden panelling, a hole in forehead and chest.

The corpse heaved himself up out of the coffin and crossed to the slumped figure. 'I knew you couldn't resist coming to check that I was finally dead.'

He sheathed his gun, picked up the new corpse and with a little difficulty dumped it in the casket. Then he took a candle over to the vestry where the flickering light revealed a priest tied to a chair. The resurrected man dropped a small wad of bills on the table. 'That's a donation to church funds.' He counted out some coins. 'And that should be enough to pay the gravedigger. The deceased doesn't need a coffin; he's already got one. If you want a name you can put Billy Shuttle on the marker.'

At the entrance he passed a bill over to the old woman. 'That's for your trouble, ma'am, and for coughing when the critter came in.' He moved through the doorway, settled his hat on his head and breathed deep of the night air. 'By the way,' he said to the lady before he left, 'there's a priest back there who'd appreciate some untying.'

And with a touch of his hatbrim – and a 'Goodnight, ma'am,' he was gone.

Mississippi Fats moved from saloon to saloon keeping an eye out for suckers willing to risk the farm on a few hands of poker. He didn't play cards, he played people. Way back before the war, on the Mississippi steamboats he had learned to read the other man's eyes. You don't listen to him; you don't stare at your cards. You watch his eyes and read what they tell you.

But he knew better than to ride into a new town and take the first sucker he saw. No point in fleecing a local big noise with the possibility of his having pistol-packing pals round every corner. For that you needed a fast gun and a fast horse. He didn't know one end of a gun from the other and his horse couldn't go anywhere fast, not with the tonnage Fats carried. So, when he rode into a place new to him, he bided his time, getting to know who was who in town; who were locals with dangerous muscle; and who were strangers, defenceless and ready for plucking.

He'd been in Comfort Creek a couple of weeks now and had got the lie of the land. He had time to kill. And that's how come he knew the guy sitting on the other side of the table was a safe target: a stranger riding through. As he'd always told himself: if you don't see a sucker at the table, you're it. And this bozo was a sucker all right – a cattleman who'd pulled off a big deal and was fool enough to let everybody know.

With the brim of his own Stetson pulled low to obscure his own eyes, Fats could read the man like a book. Within a few hands he could tell when the guy was bluffing or had got some weight in his hands. The fellow was easy meat. He fell for the distracting chatter, and for Fats's ploy of letting him win small pots while the master slowly raised the ante.

But Fats had enough sense not to completely cream the man. The downside of playing a stranger to town lay in what you *didn't* know about him. So you didn't push him too far.

Just for the hell of it, Fats bluffed on a bad hand. He knew the other had a fistful of good cards, but he also knew the fellow was prone to collapse whenever it got critical. The poor guy couldn't take pressure and really shouldn't be sitting at a card-table.

Through the smoke, Fats noted the sweat mounting on the man's brow, the concern in the eyes, the edgy way he fingered his cards. With a professional interest in how much it would take for this particular bozo to crack, he pushed up the stakes, relentlessly like a loco building up a full head of steam. He learned the guy's breaking-point was two yards – when the man folded with 200 bucks on the table.

He offered the fellow another game and, when the man declined as he expected, he thanked him for his company and wished him better luck next time. He bought the crestfallen fellow a drink, then went to the faro-table.

An hour later he had another fifty to add to the night's take when he heard the barman shout, 'Come on, guys. Ain't you got homes to go to?'

Fats looked at the banjo clock on the wall and then around the room, noting the place was nearly empty. He downed the dregs of his glass, bade the few remaining customers goodnight and stepped out onto the boardwalk.

He lit a cheroot and leant on the rail, contemplating the balmy night air. It had been a fair evening's work. In his day he'd won card-games with pots bigger than a horse could jump over, so $250 was no great shakes. But it would keep the wolf from the door until...

Yeah, until...

He mused on what lay ahead. Yeah, a month from now he would have enough dough to see him through to the end of his days. And he wouldn't have to scratch his living at the card-table. He would carry on playing cards, it was in his blood, but from then on he could do it at his leisure, just for sport.

Satisfied with his thoughts and anticipations, he flicked the butt into the road and headed towards his lodgings. Catering for drummers, it was not quite the best place in town. Not to fret, he mused, from a month's hence to the day they put him under, it would be nothing but the best.

But for the meantime, this place would suffice. One thing he liked was his comfort and, although he had to put up with the drone of drummers talking business, at least the establishment stretched to offering hot baths and the meals were good. Before turning in he would avail himself of the facilities, taking a last drink with biscuits and a hunk of cheese.

But he never got there. Within a block of his destination, a rifle cracked and his vast mass pitched forward to thud hard against the planks of the boardwalk.

'Turned up something that might be important, chief.' It was Comfort Creek's deputy sheriff who was speaking. He'd just returned to the law office after spending a chunk of the morning going round town asking questions. 'Storeowner at the end of the drag says he heard hoof-beats just after the shooting. Somebody seemed to be heading out of town mighty quick.'

The sheriff absorbed the information. 'Well, that's good news.'

'Good news? Don't understand, chief?'

'It means the killer ain't in town. That's

less work for us.' This was the first killing in Comfort Creek's ten years' existence. The most that the lawmen had to contend with were drunks and the occasional scrap; fact was, once you were used to a quiet life, you wanted it to stay that way. 'All we gotta do is notify county headquarters,' he went on, taking a form from his drawer. 'Anybody see the guy?'

'No, chief.'

The sheriff contemplated the blank sheet, then went to the stove and filled two tin mugs from the steaming pot. 'When you've had a coffee, go back round town. See if you can find out if anyone is aware of somebody who's suddenly missing – a stranger, anybody.' He nodded to the form on his desk. 'If we can get some kind of description we can add that to our report.'

He took his mug back to the desk and sat down. 'One thing we know. That guy stretched out in the funeral parlour had over three hundred bucks in his wallet. So whoever did it, the motive sure wasn't robbery.'

TWO

Tyler Morse had been minding his own business over a drink when he heard a familiar voice behind him. 'Jeez, am I glad to find you.'

He turned and saw a man with a scar which ran so close to his eye, it pulled the eyelid out of whack. 'Denver, old pard. Well, doggone!'

He slapped the back of the fellow. 'Gee, it's real great to see you. How long you been in Jacksburg?'

'Rode in a short whiles back. Been looking for you ever since I hit town.'

'What are you drinking?'

'A snort of whiskey will do me.' He looked back at the door. 'But more important, is there someplace we can talk?'

Tyler nodded to the empty end of the saloon.

'What's this all about?' he said when he eventually joined his friend, putting a couple of glasses on the table.

Denver knocked his drink back in one go. 'You heard about Little Billy Shuttle and Mississippi?'

'I heard about Little Billy. Got gunned down in some church a few weeks back. Poor Billy. Mighty strange circumstance that.'

'Well, the same's happened to Mississippi.'

Concern came to the older man's face. 'Where? When?'

'Three days ago. Over in Comfort Creek. It's in the paper.' Denver drew a cutting from his pocket and laid it on the table in front of the other man. 'There. It gives all the details. Got gunned down in the street just after playing cards.'

Tyler shrugged. 'Well, Mississippi knew how to relieve a man of his wherewithal. Maybe he'd had a good win and somebody was getting his dough back. Or maybe it was straight robbery. Mississippi always carried a wad.'

'He'd been playing cards all right. But it wasn't robbery. See, it tells you there. He'd still got a full wallet.'

Tyler cast his eyes down the piece. 'Hell, that's too much of a coincidence. First Little Billy, now Mississippi.'

'You're telling me. And it's danged obvious what's going on. That bozo Copperhead is knocking us all off. You know how unpredictable he is.'

'Have they caught him?'

'Not as far as I know. Ain't heard nothing about 'em nailing him. Anyways, how are they to know it's him? Ain't no witnesses. There's only us to put two and two together. We're the only ones who can put the finger on him.'

'Jeez, this is scary. What do you suggest?'

'Only one thing for it. We gotta get him before he gets us.'

Tyler returned to the bar and bought a bottle. He slopped whiskey into the two glasses. 'We ain't no good with guns, Denver.

Hell, even the rabbits would be safe if we went a-hunting. We go looking for him and we'll get kill't a hell of a lot quicker.'

'Well, what can we do, Tyler?'

'Nothing for it; we just gotta make ourselves scarce, keep out of his way.'

'Running ain't the answer. You know Copperhead; he's as ornery as a one-eyed mule. Once he's got an idea in his head, ain't nothing gonna stop him. He's already put lead in two of our gang. It's plain he's a-fixing to bury us too and collect for himself. He'll get us sooner or later.'

Tyler thought on it. 'We could pay a gunslinger to get him. I know there's guns for sale. If you know where to look.'

'With what? I figure they don't hire cheap. Have you got the kind of jack to pay a gunny? I sure ain't.'

Tyler mused further. 'No. But we *could* have. If we head up to Fargo and collect our due before Copperhead gets there. Then we'd have enough dough to pay an *army* to plant him.'

Tyler Morse was lying on his bed thinking things through when there was a knock at the door. He pulled the gun from its holster hanging on the headboard of the bed, rose and stood by the side of the door. 'Yeah?'

'The sheriff. Let me in.'

'How do I know who you are?' Tyler queried.

'It's the sheriff all right,' came another voice from the corridor. 'And I'm his deputy.'

Tyler felt a little safer. He didn't recognize either. And Copperhead didn't have a partner so there would only have been one voice anyway.

'OK, come in,' he said, unlocking the door.

'You're mighty jumpy, ain't you,' the sheriff said when he had entered and noted the gun in Tyler's hand.

'Can't be too careful, Sheriff,' he explained, sitting back on the bed and returning the gun to its holster. 'What's this all about?'

'First things first. What's your name?'

'Tyler Morse. Now, what's it all about?'

'Is that your pardner over at the drovers' quarters?'

'Which one?'

'The guy you been seen talking with in the saloon. Got a bad scar pulling his eyelid down.'

'Sounds like a friend of mine, yeah. Name of Denver Pike.'

'Well, I got some bad news, pal. He's just been shot.'

'Jeez,' Tyler exclaimed, consternation breaking out across his features as he leapt to his feet. 'How bad is he?'

'The baddest. Got more holes in him than a woodpecker's nest.'

Tyler fell back on the bed, his head in his hands. 'Jeez, Jeez.'

The sheriff watched the distraught figure for a moment. 'Judging by the way you're taking this, I figure you and him were close?'

'Not close, not like brothers or anything. But buddies, yeah. He was a regular guy.' He took a handkerchief and wiped his face.

'I'm gonna miss him for sure, but truth of the matter is, Sheriff, that ain't the main reason I'm taking it bad.'

'Go on.'

'I'm next on the list,' Tyler said agitatedly. 'I gotta get out of town.'

'You ain't going no place until you've answered a few questions,' the sheriff said. 'You're talking like you know who did it.'

Tyler didn't seem to hear the lawman. 'First Billy,' he whimpered, 'then Mississippi. Now poor Denver. It's me next for sure. Jeez.'

The sheriff harrumphed noisily. 'You're talking in riddles, my friend,' he said, dropping into a chair. 'Better tell me all you know.'

Tyler's mind seemed to return to the conversation. 'It's Copperhead.'

The sheriff shook his head in frustration. 'From the beginning.'

'There was five of us. We were workmates, punching cows.'

'When I came in, couldn't help but notice you got a game leg,' the sheriff said. 'Can't picture you riding herd.'

'No, that was before. Had a horse fall on me. Then went to work in the livery. But I still knew the other guys and we would meet up when they were in town. Have a drink, play a few hands of poker, that kind of thing. Then one game got serious. I've always said you shouldn't play for big dollars with friends. Ain't politic. But it happened one pay-day and Copperhead dropped a pile.

'Well one of us, Mississippi Fats, was a real whizz with cards and Copperhead got it into his skull Mississippi had organized the rest of the guys together to gyp him. Hell, we wouldn't do that. We were all pals. Anyways, he turned nasty.'

He twirled his finger around the side of his forehead. 'See, Copperhead's a bit loco. Had some kind of bang to the head when he was a kid or som'at. Anyways, now and again he loses all reason. He said he was gonna kill us all. Well, we managed to scatter and I thought he would calm down like he normally did. But I think his brain's real gone now. He's got two of the guys already. First he got Billy down at Morgan's Crossing. Then tonight Denver told me he got Mississippi over in Comfort Creek. Both of them were recorded in the papers. You can check the facts.'

He wiped his brow again. 'Why, me and Denver was discussing the matter this very evening. That's why I was cagey when you came a-knocking.' He reflected and grunted, 'Seems like I got good reason to be cagey. From what he's done to poor Denver, it's plain Copperhead's already in town.'

The sheriff nodded. 'Yeah, I can see why you're jittery. This Copperhead, what's his full name. What's he look like?'

'Copperhead Andrews. Hails from Kentucky. Big fellow. Usually wears a hat with a snake's rattler in the band. Rattles when he moves his head. Don't know his born given name but figure he's called Copperhead because of his hair. You can't miss it. Massive shock of blond hair. But when you get to know him, the moniker ties in better with his character – him being as dangerous as a copperhead snake.'

The sheriff took in the facts. 'Listen, we can protect you.'

'How many deputies you got?'

'Just the one. Bert here.'

'One?' Tyler grunted. 'Ain't enough. Mighty obliged for the offer, Sheriff, but you don't know Copperhead. 'Sides, I gotta be moving on anyhows. If that's OK with you.'

'When you aiming to leave?'

'Now the varmint's in town I figure my life ain't worth a brass nickel. I gotta leave tonight.'

The sheriff thought on it. 'Maybe that's for best. I can see the spot you're in. OK, you got my blessings to go but, when you've saddled up, come over to the law office so we can take more details of this Copperhead guy. Maybe between now and then you can remember more so you can give us a fuller description of him.'

'Anything you say, Sheriff.'

The lawman noticed the jitters in the

man's voice. 'Tell you what. I'll set my deputy Bert here to ride out with you to the town boundary, or even the county border if you're that worried. That should give you safe passage out of Jacksburg and my bailiwick. Bert'll hang about a spell, too, check you're not being followed.'

'Much obliged, Sheriff.'

THREE

Gage City was a settlement of forty-seven souls all of whom would rather be elsewhere. It was three years since the town had been established in anticipation of the railroad coming through. Stores, saloons and other amenities had been built. A name sign was erected at the entrance to town, proudly proclaiming the population figures. At first the number was regularly painted over as the population expanded to 100, then to over 200.

However, in the event, the tracks had missed them by thirty miles and everything had gone downhill. The footloose ones – those who hadn't sunk everything into the place – were the first to go when it was clear the rail-boom was not going to materialize. For a while the population sign was still painted over as the number turned and fell, but the job had been given up long since and the dust-covered numeral now stood erroneously at ninety-five.

There was little economic activity other than servicing local farms. So, although to a newcomer, it might momentarily give the outward appearance of a thriving community, fact was, it had nothing to thrive on.

And none knew that more than Gentry Jones. Back in the early days he had read about the new town and journeyed out to look the place over when it was a hive of activity. A blacksmith by trade, he had quickly noted the town was still shy of a smithy. Seeing an opportunity, he talked it over with his new bride and they moved out not long after the establishment of the community. They sunk their savings into building a place. It was expensive as wood out in the middle of nowhere was at a premium. But they reckoned it was worth the gamble. So they had a smithy with domestic quarters above and at the back, together with a wagon and a couple of horses.

But now it was all he could muster to finance meagre meals for their table. And with his only assets being the building and equipment, he couldn't up his picket-pin and head out.

He stepped out into the street and glanced at the fading sun as he locked the doors after yet another unpressured day. Walking round the back, he washed at the pump and clumped into the kitchen.

'How's the day been, dear?' his wife asked him as she kissed him on the cheek. 'I could hear your hammer clanging.'

She was delicately featured with auburn hair. When they had first gone out walking together all those years back in St Jo he had found it hard to believe such a beauty would have allowed him to pay her court. But the strain of the last few years had made its mark and the look of carefree happiness that had first enraptured him had faded from her eyes.

He returned her kiss and sat at the table.

'Repairing one broke buggy wheel. Then fixing the hinges on a wagon tailboard. That's all the work that came my way by noon so I spent the afternoon making shoes.' Unable to sit around doing nothing, he always used spare time to build up his stock of horseshoes. But he was at a point where he had more shoes than he knew what to do with.

'Don't worry, dear,' she said, as she placed a plate on the table before him. 'Something will turn up.'

He chuckled. 'Yeah, we'd be OK if the Seventh Cavalry came through and wanted all their hosses shoeing!'

He considered the plate, brimming with meat and potatoes. 'Marybelle, you're a gem. This smells great. And how you manage to put such meals together on the cents I'm pulling in, I'll never know.'

'All I can say,' she smiled as she took up position opposite him, 'is don't look too carefully at the meat. It's not the best of cuts.'

'In that case you're a miracle worker, honey. There'd be no complaints if this was served in some swank hotel.'

He was helping her with the dishes at the end of their meal when there came a knock at the door. Gentry recognized the leather-faced man in cap and bulky jacket as a homesteader from one of the outlying plots.

'Sorry to disturb you at this hour, Gentry,' the caller said, 'but I was fixing to ride out to my brother's over in the next county. I got some urgent family business out there. But when I checked my hoss over I found he needs a couple of shoes.'

'You got him here?'

'No. I was a-feared to ride him. One shoe's loose and he's completely throwed the other. You'll have to come out.'

'OK, I'll come in the morning.'

'Snag is, it's a long ride out to my brother's and I was aiming to leave a spell before dawn. So, if you can oblige me, it'll have to be now or real early tomorrow.'

Gentry looked at the darkening sky. 'Don't

cotton to leaving the missus in the evening.'

'It'll be best to get it out of the way now,' his wife said, coming to his side. Overhearing the conversation she did not want to be the reason for him not earning much needed extra money.

He put his arm round her. 'You sure, Marybelle? It'll take a couple of hours.'

'Gentry Jones, I'm a growed woman. I can look after myself.'

'OK, if you're sure.' He kissed her forehead and looked back at his visitor. 'I'll get my tack and load the wagon.'

He smelled it before he saw it.

The job had taken longer than he had anticipated and he was now returning home. Marybelle had probably gone to bed by now. The homesteader's horse had smaller hoofs than he had anticipated and, although the smith had taken a range of shoes, he had to do some fixing to get a couple down to size.

During the return journey he had let the horses set their own pace in the darkness.

The late hour and the regular creak of the wagon had prompted his eyes to close for brief spells.

It was the smell of smoke that first hit him. Downwind of the town, he blinked his eyes open and looked ahead to make out a glow. Hell of a fire to be seen from this distance. Bad trouble for somebody, he thought.

It was another fifteen minutes before he was making the approach to town. And as he got closer he began to feel some concern. The conflagration was on the near side of the settlement, where his place was. He gigged the horses. Given all the structures were of wood and close together there could be trouble. Every pair of bucket-wielding hands would be needed and he had to get back as soon as possible. Even more, if the fire were on his side of the street he would need to damp down the walls of his place as soon as possible.

But when he came in sight of the main drag, his concern turned to panic. It was *his* place burning!

He slewed the wagon round and leapt from the seat before the horses had stopped. Somebody grabbed the harnesses and sought to calm the animals as Gentry dashed towards the building. It was still recognizable as his home but the interior was ablaze and flames tongued towards the night sky.

He pushed by the chain of townsfolk engrossed in passing buckets along to be thrown on the conflagration. 'Marybelle!' he yelled. 'Where's Marybelle?'

'It's Gentry,' someone shouted.

He grabbed one of the men. 'Where's Marybelle?'

'I'm sorry, Gentry,' the man muttered.

'Sorry? What the hell does that mean?'

In the frantic activity there was no reply. He raised his hands to shield his face and moved tentatively towards the building. But he was held back from plunging into the inferno by grabbing hands.

'I've got to save her!' he yelled.

'It's too late,' one of his restrainers said.

'You mean...'

'Yeah, she didn't survive.'

He was pulled away and escorted slowly down a block. One of the men pointed to a blanketed-covered figure on the boardwalk. 'I'm sorry, Gentry.'

Hesitantly, he stepped up onto the planking and knelt before the shape; but restraining hands prevented him from pulling away the blanket. 'I shouldn't look, Gentry.'

He didn't need to. He could see a blackened hand protruding from the covering.

'She managed to get out,' a man said. 'But she was – well, all ablaze. We did what we could but...'

Gentry took the small hand but the skin was black and hard. He hesitated to think what the once beautiful face beneath would look like.

'What started it?' he whispered eventually.

'Don't know. Nobody saw it until it was an inferno.'

Gentry cursed himself and his job. He was aware of the hazards and always took care. But working with fire all day there was always the chance of a smouldering ember ending up somewhere and then slowly and surreptitiously effecting its deadly work once doors were locked.

'I know it ain't much,' somebody said, 'but we managed to get your wagon and horses clear.'

'Oh, you got wagon and horses clear,' Gentry snarled, whirling round. 'Well, that's all right then.'

The speaker dropped his head in his hand, realizing his tactlessness. His own brain in confusion, he had merely sought some comforting comment for his neighbour. And he had come up with something stupid.

He sat in the church among faces, faces once familiar now inexplicably strange. The words coming from the pastor at the front were just noise. Gentry was not a regular churchgoer so it was impossible for him to be in such a place without remembering the church back in St Jo when they were married.

Oblivious of his surroundings, his mind wandered. If only he hadn't talked her into coming out here, a rough wilderness where fatality lurked around every commonplace corner. Rattlesnakes, epidemics, lack of doctors, lawlessness – indeed, fire. Maybe if he hadn't have been so wide-eyed in his optimism, so fired up with the possibilities of a new life in paradise … Maybe if he had been more careful, had been more thorough in his checking for sparks before he had closed the smithy door...

He felt further guilt in the fact that he hadn't cried since the tragedy. He couldn't understand it. From the moment he had seen the blanketed figure of his loved one and known it was irretrievably all over, a strange numbness had descended on him. No tears, a nothingness. As though he was no longer a human being, merely a shell.

Thus, in a resigned and hopeless away he followed the coffin to the cemetery. His eyes still dry he watched as it was lowered into the ground. Back in town, fellow mourners gave final condolences and left him to his sorrow.

A neighbour had given him use of a room. They gave him some tea but said nothing when, after a couple of sips, he rose and headed for the door. Realizing his need to be alone they kept their distance.

He trudged up the stairs, the numbness that had swathed him since the accident gradually becoming a confusion of thought and emotion. Mechanically, he turned the knob and entered the room. With the door shut behind him, the outside world at last at a distance, he broke down and wept like he'd never done in his life.

Two hours on he was still prostrate on the bed. He couldn't rest. Nothing for it but to throw himself into work. Work? What work? He had no workplace!

But he had to do *something*.

He removed the borrowed suit and, like a soldier donning his helmet before an engagement, he pulled on his everyday clothes. He refreshed his face with water from the bowl in his room, then slowly descended the stairs, breathing brokenly like some sufferer of consumption. Till dark he toiled at salvaging what he could from the burned-out wreck. The charred timbers that he stacked at the side and the tools he reclaimed were unimportant in themselves. But the activity was a way in which he could, maybe, lose himself.

FOUR

'Every man drinks to forget.'

The man's eyes wandered falteringly around the room, his finger sweeping vaguely across the scene. It was late evening in the *Billy-Be-Damned*, Gage City's one surviving drinking parlour.

'See those bozos?' he went on. 'Trying to forget they're low-paid punchers or dirt-farmers without the dough to maintain a wife, that's what.' His hand wavered uncertainly in the direction of a couple of dark-suited men against the bar and he laughed. 'And them? Store traders. Now, I guess, they *can* afford a woman – but they're trying to forget the stone-faced crows they're saddled with back in the parlour!'

He laughed again and took a long draught from his glass. Then his demeanour became more serious. 'And me?' He patted his game leg and, to demonstrate his point, he moved it slightly, grimacing as he did so. 'I'm drinking, trying to forget this son of a bitch. Hell, since the Lord in his wisdom inflicted this on me, ain't been no good to man nor beast.'

His bleary eyes moved in Gentry's direction. 'And you, feller? What you trying to forget?'

Gentry grunted and eventually said, 'That I once had the most beautiful wife in the world.'

'And she left you. Yeah, I know. It's an old story, kid. Hell, you can't trust females. You know–'

He got no further in his blathering as Gentry's strong hand shot out and gripped his forearm. 'Don't you talk like that, stranger. My woman didn't *leave* me. She was *took*.'

Even in his inebriety the older fellow realized he had touched a raw nerve and remained silent, letting the words hang in the air.

Eventually Gentry let go and pointed skyward. 'She got took, God bless her. By Him up there.'

'Jeez, I'm sorry, feller.'

Silence reigned further until the man, still trying to rub life back into his arm, said, 'That's sure one hell of a grip you got there, feller. What do you do? Throw dwarves for a living?'

'Comes from wielding a thirty-pound hammer.' Gentry threw a large mouthful down his throat. 'On top of losing my missus, I've lost everything – my livelihood, all my worldly goods – save the clothes on my back and some loose change in my pockets.'

'Jeez, how come?'

'Trade's a blacksmith. Couple of days ago my smithy went up in flames. You can see it at the end of the street.' He emptied his glass and grunted; a hard, sardonic grunt. 'You can't miss it. It's the pile of charred wood in between the general store and the horse doctor's.'

'It happened that recent? Jeez, I'm real sorry, feller. I'm a stranger in town. I didn't know.' His eyes showed that the scale of the fellow's personal disaster had made some impact on him. He staggered upright and took hold of the two empty glasses. 'Boy, you *do* need a drink. This one's on me.'

Sleep now was always slow in coming. And when it came it provided no respite. Layers of nightmares that erupted in an ugly, reddened glow. And he would wake, shivering, wet with sweat...

It was mid-morning and Gentry had been working at what remained of his smithy since sun-up. Besmirched with soot, he grabbed the end of a beam and pulled. Once it was clear he hauled it to the side of the site and dropped it alongside a stack of similarly charred timber.

'That must have been one hell of a fire.'

He turned to see a man watching him. There was something vaguely familiar about the silver-haired oldster. Then he recognized him as the fellow with whom he had spent some time the previous evening.

'Sorry about shooting my mouth off about women and such last night,' the man went on. 'I'd had a bit to drink. I didn't know. I'm a stranger in town.'

Gentry gave him a glance and carried on with his work. 'Think nothing of it, pal. You weren't to know.'

'Anything you can salvage?' the man continued.

Gentry wiped his forehead with a jet-black hand and, indicated the growing stack of timber. 'Should be able to get a few dollars for this lot as kindling. The brick oven is still standing. And the anvil should be under there somewhere.' He kicked at a pile of blackened tools as he returned to the centre of the remains. 'Metal tools, of course. They came through blacked up a mite but unscathed. They're still usable – or saleable.'

'Seems to me you could do with a helping hand, young feller,' the man said, moving forward, hand outstretched. 'Name's Morse. Tyler Morse.'

The blacksmith paused in his task and looked the man over, finally responding with his own name. 'Gentry Jones.' He declined the handshake, grimacing at his dirty hand by way of explanation. 'But what about your leg?'

'It's a bind, no denying, but I ain't a complete cripple.'

'I can't pay you.'

'You can stand me a drink, can't you?'

Somewhere underneath the face, striped with black and sweat, Gentry smiled a little. 'Thanks.'

'You ain't getting in my tubs looking like that.' The speaker was a wiry-looking Chinaman with hardly a trace of Asian accent.

It was late afternoon and the two men were calling it a day. They had just entered the communal bathing facility, an open-air enclosure surrounded by a high fence beside the laundry.

'Take your duds off,' the washman instructed, 'and I'll give you a dousing before you climb in.' The water that he poured over them was cold but, before they clambered into one of the tubs, he added a few pails from the large cauldron bubbling in the centre of the complex.

'You want I should launder your duds?' the Chinaman asked.

'Not mine,' Gentry said. 'I'll be messing 'em up tomorrow just as bad.'

The two men wallowed silently in the luxury for a while, the water cleansing while relaxing their tired muscles.

'That must have been bad,' Gentry commented, noting the discoloured serrations along Tyler's leg as the old man wiped it with a towel after they had clambered naked out of the tub.

'Danged hoss fell on me. Bust the thing.' He fingered the scar. 'And that scarring is where some buckle on the hoss's rig cut into me.'

The talk continued as they completed

their ablutions. Gentry learned that the two men were separated by more than age. While he was a townie, knowing only St Jo back East and his life as a smith in Gage City, Tyler was a much-travelled Westerner. They took a meal together, finishing up in the *Billy-Be-Damned*, where the older man regaled his companion from his seemingly endless fund of tales.

The next day followed the same pattern with the two men working together, continuing the demolition of the smithy. Mid-morning, one of the townswomen brought them lemonade and fresh-made biscuits.

'Folks are real friendly round here,' Tyler said as they sat on a reclaimed beam, taking their refreshment.

'As the town's population dwindled,' Gentry said, 'folks seemed to become more close-knit. You know, like they're all sharing the same troubles. And, with fewer neighbours, it's easier to remember names!' He went on to explain the town's economic misfortunes.

'And are folks still leaving?' Tyler asked.

'Yeah,' Gentry replied, looking up and down the street. 'Don't know what future it's got.'

'You gotta face it, kid. In a short spell this could be a ghost town. I seen a few of them in my time. All over the West, north and south. Dead towns without a living soul, save a few scavenging coyotes. And no movement discernible to the eye, save tumbleweeds blowing along the drag and smashed doors swinging on broken hinges. Real, eerie places. It can happen anywhere. A string of bad seasons, or folks don't happen to build in the right place.'

He looked up and down the street. 'This place could go the same way. You given any mind to what you're gonna do then?'

Gentry grunted. 'Huh, ain't given mind to what I'll be doing next week!'

FIVE

The proprietor crossed the floor of the *Billy-Be-Damned*. It was nine o'clock in the morning. The place reeked of spilled booze and stale smoke from the night before. He unlocked the doors and pulled them back. He clipped them to the wall and looked over the batwings to check that the town was still there. The town was there all right – and so was Gentry Jones. The smith had been leaning against the outer wall of the saloon and had been spurred into movement by the clatter that meant opening time.

'Morning, Gentry.'

The blacksmith returned the greeting as he pushed through the batwings.

'You're getting earlier and earlier, kid. Hardly ever seen you in here, now you're turning into one of my best customers.'

Gentry wiped his brow. 'Been slaving for an hour. Thought it time to take a break and a snort. You any objections?'

'That's what I'm here for,' the proprietor said. 'You'll have to be patient. It'll take me a few minutes to get the place going.' He crossed to a window and opened it to freshen up the premises.

Gentry took the chairs from a table, placed them in position round the table and took residence in one. 'Take your time.'

Across the way, Tyler Morse had checked out of the hotel and collected his horse from the livery. He walked it over to the saloon, tied the animal to the rail and entered. 'Thought I'd catch you in here,' he said, spotting Gentry, now with a second whiskey in hand.

'Take a drink?' Gentry asked.

'Too early for me, pal. Besides, I want a clear head; I got some riding to do.'

'Riding? You're leaving? Just when I was beginning to enjoy your company.'

'Yeah. Gotta make tracks. Fact is, I just

dropped in to say *adios*.'

'Where you heading?'

'Dunno. Fact is, it ain't a matter of where I'm heading, more a matter that I shouldn't be here.'

Gentry lowered his voice. 'Sounds like you're on the run.'

Tyler grunted at the notion. 'Suppose I am in a way, but not the way you mean.' He stuck out his hand. 'Anyways, enjoyed your company too. Hope our tracks will cross again sometime.'

Gentry reciprocated. 'And thanks for helping me out. It's been good to have someone to talk to. Helped take my mind off things.'

Tyler nodded. 'Anytime, pardner. You been through hell. I hope things turn out for you.'

He touched his hat and was gone.

'Good guy,' Gentry said, making for the bar for a refill.

'Didn't know him long enough,' the proprietor said. 'But the short time he was in town, he didn't give me no reason to complain.'

Outside, Tyler checked the cinch and other fastenings. Satisfied everything was in order, he mounted but instead of pulling away he sat contemplatively in the saddle. After some moments, he dismounted, retethered his horse and returned to the *Billy-Be-Damned.*

Inside, the sense of the place being still asleep was being dispelled, with a handful of customers now bellying up to the bar for refreshment.

'Gee, that was quick,' Gentry smiled, spotting Tyler coming through the door. 'Long time no see.'

'I will take a drink after all,' Tyler said. He nodded to Gentry's near-empty glass. 'Another?'

'Won't say no.'

'I'd just got my ass in the saddle when I had an idea,' Tyler went on in a low voice when they were seated together each with a full glass. 'It occurred to me there might be a way that we could be useful to each other. Me with my problem and you being a smith.'

'You got a problem?'

'Yeah, but I can tell you about that in a minute. First, this dreadful thing that's happened to you. I ain't very good with words so don't get me wrong at what I'm about to say.'

Gentry nodded. 'OK'

'This bad thing, I know it's something you'll never get over, but you think you might move to a time when you can start to put it behind you? You know, think of the future?'

'What you talking about?'

'I've asked you before and I'm gonna ask again. What you aiming to do now?'

'Get what cash I can from that burnt-out hulk, then – I don't know.'

'We've only knowed each other a couple of days but I think you're a regular guy, Gentry. Somebody I could trust. The kind I could work with. Like I said, I've got this idea.'

'I think this is what's called beating about the bush,' Gentry said. 'For hell's sake,

Tyler, spit it out.'

Tyler turned, noting more customers coming in. 'Let's find somewhere quiet. Over at the smithy should be private enough.'

'What I'm gonna tell you,' he continued when they were out of earshot of anybody, 'you gotta promise, if nothing comes of it, you don't tell nobody.'

'I'm a simple craftsman, Tyler. You ought to know that by now.'

'That's the way I've pegged you.'

'So, I don't want to cause anybody any trouble. Especially a good friend like yourself. Whatever you tell me stays with me.'

Tyler looked at him with a narrowness and intensity of focus; and liked what he saw in the other's eyes. 'Yeah, I believe you. You're a regular guy.'

He built a smoke and began. 'You're quite right about me being on the run, Gentry. But it ain't from the law. There's this crazy man who's been knocking off certain folk. He's dropping us one by one like he's playing ninepins. There's only one left. Me. And I'm next. That's why I'm moving on. The bozo's got a nose for sniffing out folks's where-at. So what I need is somebody who can look after himself and *me*.'

'Listen, if it's a bodyguard you're after I'm not really your man. Just 'cos I'm big and beefy, don't mean I'm a fistfighter. Last time I had a scrap was in the school yard. And I ain't no Westerner either. Sure, I know where the trigger is on a gun, but that's about all. There wasn't much call for developing expertise in gunplay back in St Jo.'

'There's more to this business than that.'

'The more you talk, the less I understand.'

'I'll start at the beginning so you can get the whole picture. Me and Denver Pike had a livery stable back in Beauville. It was near the end of the war and late one night a small detachment of Confederates rolled in. They were bushed and decided to bivouac overnight in town. They had a wagon and commandeered our stable to store it. At the time it didn't occur to nobody to ask why they should need to store it under cover. Anyways, come morning they were about to pull out when Union forces turned up. Although the Rebs were only some half-dozen, they resisted and for half an hour the town was a battlefield. When the dust cleared, the Rebs were dead to a man. It was clear the Union soldiers didn't know about the wagon because after the skirmish they pressed on.

'When they'd gone me and Denver decided to have a look inside it. Then we knew why the Rebs wanted to store it in the barn. It wasn't that it should be under cover away from the elements – they wanted to *hide* it. It was full of gold bars! As you know, the Confederacy was seeking all kind of routes to get money across the border in payment for arms. This had been one of the shipments.

'We were deciding what to do with it when Copperhead and his bunch bust through the doors. He and his gang – Three-Fingers Lassiter, Mississippi Fats, Little Billy Shuttle – were just scavengers. They rode around seeing what they could loot. There were lots of their kind about during the war, as you might know, footloose robbers taking advantage of the general anarchy that conflict brings. Quantrill's Raiders was another one you might have heard of.'

Gentry nodded.

'Well, Copperhead and his mob had just bust in to see what he could take from the wagon – supplies, guns maybe – anything that could turn a buck. That was his business. Then he saw the gold and took over. We parleyed. He had the same idea that Denver and I was turning over. The Union didn't know about the shipment. The Reb top brass would know about it but they were being routed across the country – remember, it was near the end of the conflict. With the Confederacy collapsing around their ears the Rebs had enough on their plate at the time to worry about the where-at of just one shipment.

'On the other hand, it was a big shipment so it would only be a matter of weeks, maybe days, before some pen-pusher back in headquarters saw a hole in the books and investigators came a-looking. When that happened we figured there would be a States-wide search for the shipment. But the delay, however short, would give us time to get it out of town and magic it away someplace. We had to pick somewhere safe and act fast. The natural goal for us was the Mexican border, so that would be the focus of the authorities. And we figured that, having the telegraph they could have soldiers waiting for us anywhere along the route. So we decided to do the opposite and head for Canada. It would be a long haul but they wouldn't be looking for us up that way, at least not to start with. If we could get it across the Canadian border we would lose any US soldiers and lawmen who might be on our tail. We figured there was a bonus: that even if Washington alerted the Canadian lawmen, things being what they are between the US and the British, the Canadians wouldn't give it top priority.'

‘What I don’t understand,’ Gentry put in, ‘if this Copperhead was such a hardman why didn’t he and his bunch put you and Denver out of the way – simply bump the pair of you off – and claim the lot for themselves?’

‘I thought of that. It was odd, him putting on a show of treating us as part of his gang. We were just a couple of no-account horse-workers. But I’ve learnt enough about him since to know there’s always method in what he does. His reckoning would be, if our bodies were found in Beauville it would alert suspicions from the beginning. And if he knocked us off somewheres along the trail, it would again create suspicion and possibly give the authorities a lead in which direction the gold was going. So, for the time being, Denver and I were safe. Of course, we realized that the closer we got to the Canadian border, the less important that became and the more our lives would be at risk.

‘But then things got complicated. We knew there could be some general alert by then so we skirted townships. Anyway, we were on the home stretch – half-way across Dakota Territory – and we were bivouacking near Fargo. Well, Mississippi Fats had had the clink of poker chips in his blood since birth and the long trek had meant he had been weeks away from the game. So while we were resting up for the night he rode alone into Fargo – we didn't think a lone rider would create suspicion – to get himself a little dose of pasteboards. But he came back a mite quick, saying the scuttlebutt in the saloons all over town was that the whole territory was covered with agents looking for a missing gold shipment. How they knew, we never found out, but we must have left some clue along the way. Maybe just a gang with a wagon had been enough to arouse somebody's suspicions. Anyway, soon as we got the news we scouted round for a good place and buried it.'

'Where?'

'Not far from our bivouac near Fargo. Then we scatted, going our five separate ways.'

'And it's still there?'

'Should be.'

There was a stretch of thoughtful quiet until Gentry asked, 'How much gold was there?'

'Sixteen bars.'

'Jeez,' Gentry breathed. Then: 'But why didn't you split the gold back in Beauville and let each man take his chance then?'

'That had been my idea but I was a greenhorn in such matters. You might say, till then I'd always been on the straight and narrow. On the other hand Copperhead was a born lawbreaker and knew the ins and outs. If each man had his separate cut, he said, it wouldn't be long before one of them was found out. He knew all about owlhoots getting caught and cutting a deal for a lesser sentence, spilling the beans on their pardners. His thinking was that it was better the cache should be kept together till the heat was off. That way it was in everybody's interests to keep his trap shut.'

He ran his hand through silver-grey hair.

'So, when we'd buried it, we set a date of six months from then and lit out to all points of the compass. See, the authorities would be looking for two things. First, a gang. So that meant breaking up. Second, they would be on the lookout for a significant amount of gold mysteriously turning up someplace. On the other hand, if we were separate, and with nobody having their hands on the gold for six months, the authorities wouldn't have any leads at all. Six months on, on the agreed date, we would make our separate ways to the location, meet up and reclaim the loot.'

He rubbed his grizzled stubble. 'And that's been the way the situation's stood – until a few weeks back when the guys started getting themselves kill't.'

'What happened?'

'Well, things were going OK. I was biding my time. But then I started hearing things. See, I keep my ears to the ground, read the papers. Bad news started coming my way. First I read that Little Billy had been shot down. In a church of all places. Then my old pal Denver tracked me down in Jacksburg, asking if I'd heard about Mississippi Fats getting a dose of lead over in Comfort Creek. He was all of a shake and asking me what should we do.

'We were still pondering on it when, the very night we met up, Denver got shot up in his hotel room. Copperhead was knocking off everybody who was involved! And I was next! I really got the jitters then and lit a shuck.'

'What about the other member of Copperhead's gang? Three-Fingers something.'

'Three-Fingers Lassiter. He dropped out of the picture way back. Thin guy, always coughing. The cold got him on the journey north. I tell you, that Dakota ain't the warmest of places even in summer. We buried him someplace on the way to Fargo. I ought to have read the signs in Copperhead when Three-Fingers died. He was supposed to be a long-time pardner of Copperhead's – but the only thing Copperhead thought of when the guy coughed his last was, it was one less share in the gold.'

Gentry ruminated for a moment. 'So there's only you and Copperhead now,' he said by way of conclusion.'

'Yeah. And if he gets his way, there'll only be one – him.'

Gentry leaned back. 'What about the law in this place where Denver was killed? What did they say? What did they do?'

'They were very considerate. Seeing what was happening they put out a paper on Copperhead and escorted me out of town.'

'And where is he now?'

'Well, I ain't read of him being caught yet and I been watching my back for a month now. He's a real mean *hombre* and I had the impulse to scat – hide myself out West maybe. Then I thought no, why should I? The gold was as much mine as his. I could beat him to it.'

Gentry chewed on it, then said, 'Didn't you have any reservations about double-crossing this Copperhead? I mean, him being a gun-toting hardcase and you being an ordinary working guy?'

'Sure, but I reckoned I'd got an edge on him. His figuring would be, with me being as scared as a jack-rabbit, I'd be too concerned with hiding away and saving my skin than to think of chasing after the gold. This is where the double bluff comes in. While he's pissing around down here looking high and low for me I got a chance to get to the gold *before* him. My thinking was, if I made it, then lit out for Canada, I'd have the gold – and Canada is big enough to get lost in. Hell, with that money I could go abroad. South America. He'd never find me there.'

'Why you telling me all this?'

'Well, it'd have to be done clever. There's still gonna be army and maybe civilian law investigating.' He indicated down the street. 'I was sitting on my horse back there, getting ready to pull out of your little town, when I got the idea. For a start, I ain't no spring chicken. I'd already got a game leg. A danged horse fell on me. Left me with a couple of broken ribs that have been slow to heal. And this thing needs more than one pair of hands; I've realized that for some time. I been trying to think who do I know who would fit the bill and who I could trust. Then it hit me, just as I was about leave. You being a blacksmith and all.'

'Why a blacksmith?'

'Before we get on to that, your business being wiped out, I figure you could you use eight bars of gold. Am I right in my thinking?'

'Yes, but–'

'I don't like the but.'

'It's stealing.'

Tyler chuckled. 'You're too good to be true. Listen, it ain't gonna hurt anybody.'

'Everything belongs to someone.'

'Yeah. It belonged to the Confederacy. But the Confederacy don't exist no more! So it don't belong to anybody. It's up for grabs. It won't bring your Marybelle back. Nothing will. But you can start a new life. Gentry, in the short time we been acquainted I know that if anybody deserves a new start, you do. You got any objection to being rich?'

His words hung in the air so he threw out a prompt. 'You in?'

Gentry thought on it some more, as a positiveness entered his eyes that had not been there for a long time. 'I'm in.'

Tyler shook his hand. 'Good. Now here's the thought that came to me. Someone like you could melt down the gold and shape it in some other form, say ornaments or statues.'

Gentry became perplexed. 'Just because I know about iron, Tyler, don't mean I know anything about gold. Gold's got different properties. Needs different tools.'

'Hell, you know more about melting down metals and stuff than I do. I wouldn't have a clue how to start. Even if you ain't worked gold, with your knowledge and skills you're half-way there.'

Gentry nodded. 'I suppose it ain't all *that* different.'

'OK,' Tyler continued, 'then we could

paint the things and make out they were a shipment of ornaments or something. That way we could travel and, with a little bit of luck, get past any nosy investigators.'

'I think it might work.'

'You bet your sweet blacksmith's ass it'll work. Now, we need to split and join up again north of here. Where do you suggest? Somewhere thirty miles north.'

Gentry looked blank. 'I lived here less than three years and never travelled more than ten miles in any direction.'

Tyler shrugged. 'I got a map in my traps. Don't go away.'

Five minutes later he had returned with his horse and extracted a map from his saddle-bags which he unfurled on the ground before them. He ran his finger across the cracked varnish of the chart. 'There. Bailey's Halt.'

'Heard of it,' Gentry said, 'but never been there.'

'We'll meet up there. It's important that not too many folks link us, so I'll leave now and push west. Then I'll curve north to

Bailey's Halt and wait for you there. How long will it take for you to leave?'

'Well, I've got to sell up and get ready. Two days, maybe three.'

'Good. Don't feel the need to rush. The greater the spacing between our departures, the less anybody's going to connect us. Especially a certain bozo called Copperhead if he comes nosing in.'

'How long will it take to get up to Fargo?'

The other fingered the grey bristles on his chin. 'A month's hard riding. Maybe more. Your horses and wagon good enough for such a trip?'

'Should think so. What'll I bring?'

'Any of your tools that are gonna help in melting and reshaping gold.' He studied his companion for a moment. 'Listen, you're the technical expert on board. I ain't gonna have to spell everything out for you, am I?'

Gentry looked a mite embarrassed. 'No, no. Just give me time to get into the swing of the caper.'

Tyler built a cigarette, lit it. 'I always

remember Mississippi Fats telling me: when you're at the poker table, the only thing you know is what you're holding. What you have to figure out is – what's the other guy got.' He chuckled. 'Take that worried look off you face, kid. *We* know what we've got: *we* know where the gold is. And what's Copperhead got? The notion that I'm scatting around down here and all he has to do is knock me off, then he can take his time trekking out to claim the booty for himself in his own good time.'

He chuckled again. 'Tell you what. I'd sure like to see the look on his face when he finally gets there and sees nothing but an empty hole.'

SIX

Starting out at sun-up, it took all day for Gentry to reach Bailey's Halt. He'd got a hundred bucks in his pocket. A fortune in the circumstances. Nobody had been interested in buying what was left of the smithy. Who'd want a burnt-out hulk in the middle of a dying town? Even the ground was worthless. But he'd got a few dollars for the charred wood. There weren't many trees around Gage City and folks were willing to pay for kindling.

As he had made his goodbyes, friends had asked him his plans and he had lied, saying he didn't have any. Just aiming to find some-place where he could forget, he had told them. Lying, especially to friends, was new to him and he didn't cotton to it one bit. Being duplicitous had stuck in his craw even more when he was faced with the generosity of the folk he was leaving. Poor as they were, they had had a whip-round and he had been presented with fifty dollars in bills and coins. The dry-goods man had given him a couple of bags of horsefeed. And women loaded him with fresh-baked pies and other eatables.

So it had been with mixed feelings that he had flicked the ribbons on the horses and finally pulled out.

All day long the ironmongery had clanked behind him in the wagon. Hammers, tongs, nails and an assortment of horseshoes – all blackened but serviceable.

Was he going loco? Playing button to a crazy old-timer with a limp and talk of hidden treasure? But he had nothing to lose. What was more: whatever the outcome of this rumhead adventure, he had one thing for which to thank Tyler. The enterprise had given the young man something to think about. It was helping get his mind off his tragic loss.

Bailey's Halt was the town Gage City should have been. Setting up around the railroad station, it had blossomed into a bustling community. Rows of false fronts on either side of the drag extended right down to the rail depot. Hotels, all manner of stores, and the signs of yet new building being erected.

Part-way in he stopped the wagon and dropped to the ground. He worked the muscles of his arms and legs, as he looked the place over. It wasn't long before he saw a familiar shape hobbling towards him along the boardwalk.

'You finally made it,' Tyler said by way of greeting. 'Everything OK?'

'Yeah, apart from having no feeling in my backside.'

Tyler nodded across the street. 'We'll quarter the horses and wagon at the livery over there. Then I'll take you to the hotel where I got rooms.'

Rubbing the back of his hand over his lips, Gentry glanced up and down the street. 'Can't we talk over a drink at a saloon?'

'No. The fewer who see us together the better.'

'But I ain't had a drink since yesterday.'

Tyler eyed his companion. 'Now listen, kid, I seen you knock the head off a few jars since I knowed you – but exactly how long you been a drinking man?'

'Getting on for a week.'

'Well, it seems to be getting a fast grip on you. I want you to get one thing straight: you keep off the stuff, at least until our little venture is over. I ain't being saddled with no jughead when the chips are down. You need to keep a clear head. What you do after, how you choose to spend your half of the profit, that's up to you.'

Washed and with a full belly, Gentry was sitting on a chair in Tyler's room. The older man was laid out on the bed, smoking.

'So you got some tools,' Tyler said. 'What else do we need?'

'Working gold is different from working iron. The melting-point of gold is lower for a start, but for our purposes that's gonna be a good thing. However, the basic principles should be the same. First off, we need a furnace.'

'There's one close by to where the gold's stashed.'

'Will its owner allow us to use it?'

'Don't worry about that, kid. Don't belong to nobody. Only problem, don't know the state of it but it should be usable.'

'Right. I need gloves, thick ones. Mine were burnt in the fire. We need wood for making boxes. Sand for making the moulds. I'm new to this and might have to experiment but I figure the sand needs to be a fine texture. So whatever stuff we get, we'll still need a sieve. Then we need some kind of agent for binding the sand.'

'Such as what?'

'That's something else I'm going to have to experiment with.'

Tyler stood up and crossed to a dresser. He pulled open the top drawer and extracted a belt and holster containing a gun. He took it across to the younger man. 'Remember, part of this deal was you helping me to keep a lookout for Copperhead. I need somebody watching my back. With a bit of luck, heading north like we're doing we've left him behind. But we gotta face it, we don't know where and when he might show his ugly mug. So I want you to wear this.'

'Ain't never worn a gun-rig before.'

'There's a first time for everything.'

Gentry took the belt and strapped it round his waist. He untied the holding thong and pulled out the gun, a Navy Colt. He examined it then hefted it, testing the weight. 'Feels kinda strange.'

'You'll get used to it.'

Gentry was staring at the weapon in his hand, like it was a meteorite from Mars. 'I'm gonna need some practice if you expect me to use it.'

'Plenty of time for that. We got a long journey ahead.' Tyler pointed at the door some fifteen feet away. 'As long as you could hit that, you should be good enough.'

'From this distance I'd need two sticks of dynamite to make sure I got it. When I said I need practice – I didn't just mean with this particular model. I mean I've never actually had need to fire a gun of *any* kind before.'

Tyler's eyebrows rose. 'You've never pulled a trigger in your life?'

Gentry gingerly slipped the Colt back in its holster. 'That's about the size of it.'

'In that case, kid, it's a good thing we got a long journey ahead!'

SEVEN

With the wagon loaded they headed north, having picked up whatever useful they could at Bailey's Halt. At first Tyler rode horseback but later, with his horse in tow, he would take spells alongside Gentry on the wagon box.

Till now the draught horses had only been worked on local deliveries so the young man was aware that the animals needed time to adjust to a long haul and he didn't push them hard.

As they moved progressively into the Great Plains Gentry learned, for the first time in his life, what it was like to be a day's ride from nowhere. Often nothing from horizon to horizon in any direction.

Occasionally nights would be spent in the stables or barns of friendly farmers, but more often out in the open on the ground under the wagon. At such times each would be rolled in his own blankets, but they shared the same wagon sheet, which was why Tyler would be aware when Gentry had one of his bad dreams. At such times, if the young man didn't wake, Tyler would gently shake him out of it. But after that the young man rarely returned to sleep.

Gentry saw the seduction of the dark as untrustworthy. Weary from the day's toiling he would be lulled into sleep. But often, fiery images would take him unawares and he would wake to lie fretful, sleepless. And always the images were as strong as ever.

Nor was the day devoid of agonizing memories with its remembrances of shortcomings and the little acts of forgetfulness he could now never redress.

'I've never had a loss like you've suffered,' Tyler said once by way of comfort, 'and I'm sure you'll never get completely over it. But it might help if you try to see Gage City as your past. It's over and done. And the further you get from the place, the further back are your agonies.'

Gentry nodded although he didn't see it that way. But he knew his new friend was only trying to help.

They had just forded a shallow stream when Gentry halted the wagon and dropped down to the sandy ground of the bank. He bent down and ran some of the sand through his fingers. 'No good, far too coarse.'

He stood up and moved around, sampling more but still shaking his head.

'Keep your eyes open for fine sand,' he said as he returned to the wagon. 'We need some real fine stuff. As long as it's not too bulky we can sieve it. There must be some between here and your Fargo.'

'I'd never have thought a statue would be so hard to come by,' Tyler said. They had recently crossed The Platte and were nooning under some cottonwoods. The both of them had kept their eyes peeled for a likely model ever since they'd left Gage City. 'There must be hundreds sitting on mantelpieces all over the place, but we can't go breaking into every house between here and Fargo just to have a look.'

'I'll tell you where you should find one,' Gentry said. 'A Catholic church usually has a Madonna. That would be a suitable statue.'

Tyler pointed an ancient finger at his companion. 'Hey, the boy has brains.'

'But don't seem right,' Gentry added, having a sudden regret at making the suggestion, 'stealing from a church.'

'Listen, the Church puts charity high on its list, don't it? Well for every act of charity there has to be a recipient. In this case, *we'll* be the recipients. What's your problem?'

Gentry said nothing, which Tyler took to be acquiescence. 'Then all we got to do,' the older man went on, 'is make out that we're priests or som'at.

From then on every Catholic church or mission they passed, they dutifully paid their respects, going down the aisle, genuflecting at the altar. And Gentry had been right. Virtually every one had an effigy of Our Lady. Trouble was, they were usually in prominent positions and in excess of three feet tall.

'One of those in gold would need a crane to get it on and off the wagon,' Tyler commented. 'That's assuming the wagon could take the weight!'

They were nearing the Missouri when Tyler at last saw what he needed. In a niche in the side wall of a small chapel, a neat eighteen-inch-high heaven-sent beauty.

Back at the wagon he took out a blanket and handed it to Gentry. 'I've looked the place over. There's only the priest in there at the moment. I'll distract the guy with some heartbreaking story while you take the statue.'

'I'm no Catholic, Tyler, but I been trying to tell you, I draw the line at stealing from the Church.'

'Hell, you want a half cut in the gold, don't you? Well, you gotta earn it.'

'I'm gonna earn my cut plying my trade – smithing. That's why you roped me in, in the first place. Not for stealing from no churches.'

'Jeez,' Tyler said, as he stomped off with the blanket under his arm. 'Using an effigy of the Madonna was *your* idea.'

In frustration, he hung about outside the church. He could go in and, if confronted by the priest, act tough and just take it. It wasn't like he would be robbing a bank, so it was unlikely there'd be any gunplay. On the other hand, if the priest came out a-shouting and raising a general alarm, he might never get back to the wagon.

He watched a wedding party go in. Maybe if he mixed with the congregation he might...

No, the whole assemblage would be watching. All the same, with nothing else to do, he tagged onto the end of the group and took position in a pew, hoping that some idea would come up. While the heads of the others in attendance were directed to the front, he sat through the ceremony eying the effigy to the side of the altar. Then to his surprise and satisfaction, at the end of the service they all filed out – even the priest – to see the happy couple on their way.

Tyler saw his chance and shot along the side aisle, grabbed the statue and wrapped it in the blanket. Rather than leave by the crowded front entrance, he made for a side door. In doing so he had to pass the altar.

And as he did so he made the sign of the cross.

In gratitude.

They were nearly out of Nebraska when they were making the run-up to a small settlement.

'Good,' Gentry said. 'We need restocking with some supplies.'

They continued their approach in silence until they drew level with the town's cemetery and Tyler became mysteriously intrigued by a burial service that was taking place. 'When you've got your supplies,' he said, 'carry on riding out of town. I'll catch you up. If you see me in town before you leave, don't show you know me.'

Before Gentry could ask why, Tyler had gigged his horse towards the settlement.

By the time Gentry reached the habitation, Tyler had hitched his horse near the entrance to town and was seemingly lazing on the sidewalk with a smoke. As bid, Gentry showed no sign of recognition, and continued into the centre to conduct his purchasing.

Some quarter-hour on, Tyler watched the mourners return to town. He stepped down from the boardwalk and ground a cigarette butt into the dirt with his heel. He unhitched his horse and casually led it along the thoroughfare. Part-way down, the undertaker touched his hat and broke away from the main group to disappear into the funeral parlour. Tyler hitched his horse outside and entered the establishment.

'What can I do for you, sir?' the man asked. Unlike the usual gaunt stereotype of his occupation, he was big in both horizontal and vertical directions with a red, bulbous face.

'Can we talk in private?' Tyler asked.

'Of course, sir.' Then, with extra pomposity, he added, 'Confidentiality is a hallmark of our profession.'

'I mean, is there anybody in the place who might overhear us?'

'No, sir. Rest assured we are completely alone.'

'That's dandy,' Tyler said, pulling his gun with one hand while the other went behind his back and locked the door. 'Don't make any noise and you won't get hurt. Now, get your clothes off.'

Consternation spread across the man's features.

'Don't worry,' Tyler chuckled. 'It's just the suit I want.'

The man's quizzical eyebrows rose. 'What is this?'

'It's simple. I gotta attend an important funeral. I'm strapped for cash. I want that black suit. Now, my friend, do as I say.'

The man faltered, waved his hands over his frame and then indicated the considerable girth of the pants at belly level. 'This suit is far to big for you, sir.'

'It'll do.'

The man eyed the gun muzzle, its threatening black hole prompting him to show a more full-hearted co-operation. 'I do have one that will fit sir,' he said falteringly. 'Over there.'

'All I can see is a coffin.'

'If the gentleman will allow me,' the man said, moving cautiously towards the box. He opened the lid. 'This one would be a virtual fit.'

Tyler looked down at the lean, pasty-faced corpse. 'Yeah, it would at that. I'll take it.'

With the deceased not sharing the same need for compliance with the new customer, it took the undertaker a few minutes struggling to remove the black jacket and pants.

'Roll them up,' Tyler said when the

garments were finally being handed to him, 'and put them on the side. Then take yours off. I still want them.'

This time the man complied without question.

'And I want them all wrapped to take away,' Tyler added. 'You know, just like any good draper would do.'

Minutes later, the undertaker was in his undergarments, gagged and bound to a chair in a back room while Tyler was riding out of town.

He soon caught up with Gentry. He tossed the parcel in the back of the wagon and gigged his horse to draw level with his companion.

'What was that all about?' the young man wanted to know.

'We got our get-ups to make us look like priests, kid. Black suits – courtesy of the local undertaker.'

'You bought suits – from an undertaker?'

'Let's say – borrowed,' Tyler chuckled. 'A neat, dandy one for me, and one that will fit your big hulk better than a fancy bespoke tailor could manage.'

Gentry threw a glance back at the town. 'Jeez, Tyler. We're gonna get the law after us.'

The older man laughed. 'You think the sheriff is gonna pull a posse together to chase a couple of suits? Boy, you got a lot to learn. Anyways, did you get the supplies you needed?'

'Yes,' Gentry grunted. 'But I *paid* for my goods.'

EIGHT

Some miles further, a small train of wagons crossed ahead of them.

'Buffalo hunters,' Tyler said as the two sets of travellers exchanged waves. He watched them disappear towards the western horizon, then said, 'That gives me an idea. If everything goes to plan, when we're loaded with the statues and are heading for Canada we're gonna be disguised as priests. We've that thought out OK. But *till* that time it could be useful to have some other kind of cover.'

'That's true,' Gentry said, nodding to the rear. 'We're building up all kind of oddball stuff in the back. Any nosy coyote who chose to pry under the thin tarp might wonder what the hell we're up to.'

'That's what I been thinking,' Tyler went on. 'Now, buffalo-hides are a standard commodity in these parts. We could pick up some dirt cheap and stack them in the back. That way we'd look like buffalo-hide traders and fit better into the locale.'

They were nearing a settlement. The buildings were low and squat-roofed. The false fronts with which Gentry was familiar had not been in evidence for some time. Such erections would stand no chance against the violent winds that could sweep across the flatness of Dakota.

'We should be able to pick up our hides here,' Tyler said. He took out his map. 'Once we've crossed the line into north Dakota Territory we'll avoid habitations,' he added after some consideration. 'The place yonder will be our last port of call. So if there's anything else you need for your job, get them here.'

Gentry bit his lip thoughtfully as he checked off items on his mental list. He'd already picked up the sand he had sought, enough to fill three bags; so that was covered. 'We've got brushes and an assortment of paints, but I still need powder to make whitewash. And some large sheets of paper, say newspapers. I could do with some molasses, too.'

'OK,' Tyler said. 'I'll leave the technical stuff to you. Meantimes, we might as well stock up on some more food.'

Once they had left the town, their intention was from then on to keep away from established trails. They had been cutting across the spare, dry terrain for several hours when the sky began to darken with ugly thunderheads. So far the ominous clouds were largely behind them, while ahead the sun was still breaking through.

'With a bit of luck,' Tyler said, glancing to their rear, 'we'll keep ahead of the storm.'

But his backward look had revealed something else. 'Uh-oh,' he added. 'We're being followed.'

'How do you know?'

'I've noticed, now and again a rider has

been breaking the skyline behind us. Then he disappears like he don't want to be seen. He's there again.'

'You think it's Copperhead?'

'Too far for me to tell with any exactitude, but even at this distance I don't think it's him. Don't seem to have the build.'

Lightning crackled.

'Well, if ain't your Copperhead friend,' Gentry said, 'then I figure it's a coincidence. Just somebody heading in the same direction as us, is all. Ain't no profit in a lone rider following buffalo-hide traders.'

'That's what's concerning me. What would be the point in following us? It might be the law – or a Federal army investigator. They've been on the case from the beginning. They will have laid men off after this length of time but there's still gonna be some on the job. Tell you what: turn east at the first opportunity. Make a real sharp turn. If he does the same out here in the wilderness with no trails, then he's following us.'

Five minutes later, with the staccato sound

of lightning behind them, Gentry turned a sharp right angle and Tyler hunkered down in the back of the wagon.

'He's following us all right,' the older man said after they'd journeyed another half mile. 'Ain't no doubt.' He looked ahead and noted a stand of lonely-looking cotton-woods. 'Them trees,' he said. 'Veer a shade behind them, just enough to let me roll off without being seen. Then make sure you come back into view so he don't suspect nothing.'

At the appropriate point, Tyler dropped down and loped into cover, completing the manoeuvre quite adeptly for an old-timer with a crook leg.

Time passed, the sky darkened further, then Gentry heard a couple of cracks. Was one of them a gunshot? He looked back. Difficult to tell. Behind them a storm was letting rip and the black sky was a network of crackling white zigzags. He pulled in and turned up his collar against the first spits of rain. Seeing nothing, he jumped down, then extricated his slicker as the rain increased in intensity. He leant against the back of the wagon and squinted through the watery veil.

Maybe Tyler was right, he fretted, and the fellow wasn't the innocent Gentry supposed him to be. Maybe it was the Copperhead fellow whom Tyler had been so scared of at the beginning.

Or maybe it was someone else, someone who had seem them buy the hides in town. On the other hand, they'd been in town a long time, making purchases, taking a meal – and had left the wagon unattended. Maybe the critter had took to poking round it and underneath the buffalo trappings had seen the gear and tools and such. Not regular equipment for buffalo-hide traders. That might have roused the suspicions of someone who was already on the lookout for something odd.

He thought on the situation. The further north and the deeper into the wilderness that they had journeyed, the safer Gentry had felt. But alone in the blinding rain and unable to see his friend, he began to speculate more. It didn't have to be someone who had followed them from the outset. This might be the back of beyond but there was still a sprinkling of towns. And they weren't living in the Middle Ages. They were connected by telegraph. Authorities in the south could signal ahead and a local agent could have been delegated to pick them up and trail them.

After what seemed an eternity of turning himself into a bundle of nerves with his varied speculations, he could make out Tyler slopping through the mud towards him.

'What happened?' Gentry shouted agitatedly. 'Who was it? Was it Copperhead?'

'No. Calm down, kid.'

'So who was it?'

'Dunno,' Tyler said calmly. 'In the end the bozo didn't get close enough. Took a turn and headed north-east.' He peered in the direction he had mentioned and waved. 'You might still see him yonder.'

'I thought he might have taken a shot at you.'

'How come?'

'Thought ... maybe I heard a gunshot.'

Tyler laughed. 'Gunshot? Hell, no. A lot of thunder and lightning you heard. You were right, kid. It was a coincidence. He wasn't following us. I'm just getting too jumpy, is all, seeing him behind us like that.' In vain he tried to shake water from his saturated arms. 'And all I got for my suspicions was a damn soaking. Now, where's my slicker?'

Gentry got back onto the seat and, while Tyler rummaged about for his weather-proofs, he stared towards the north-east in search of the rider but the downpour had reduced visibility to yards. 'Just 'cos he's riding off don't mean he ain't law or something. He might be riding away to make some kind of report. Or to telegraph ahead. Anything.'

Tyler worked his head through the slicker, pulled it down and climbed back on the seat. 'Like I've said, calm down, kid. It was just a storm in a teacup.' He laughed through the rain and flicked water at the younger man. '*Storm* in a teacup, get it?'

After they had spent a damp night under a dripping wagon, the weather finally broke and by mid-morning their stuff had dried out.

Their journey continued without incident until, come noon, their passage was blocked by a line of grazing buffalo. Gentry reined in. They'd been seeing the animals increasingly over recent days but at a distance and out of the way. This was the biggest number yet.

Gentry surveyed them, stretching in both directions as far as the eye could see. 'Do we wait for them to pass or do we go round them?'

'Either way we'd lose some hours. Buffalo are harmless enough, as long as they aren't stampeded. Besides, they're strung out, not bunched. If you take it easy, we shouldn't have any trouble.'

As they resumed their progress at a slower

pace, Gentry sensed apprehension in the horses. He'd had them since he had first set up the smithy and thus was familiar with their behaviour and knew the signs. The animals had not been this close to the bulky shaggy creatures before.

In fact, neither had Gentry. He noted the piggy little eyes set in massive heads that swivelled in the direction of the intruders. After giving the interlopers an almost philosophical appraisal they returned their long-bearded chins to the more important business of grazing. Orange-coloured calves scampered for the protection of their mothers at the sight of the strange travellers.

But as Tyler had said, the animals parted in their own time, content with their munching. 'Must be the most robust critters God ever put on this earth,' he said as they moved slowly between the animals. 'When the north wind comes down bringing snow and all kinds of hell, you know what they do? They don't find shelter or hide away like we or any other sensible critter might do.

I've seen 'em. They go to the nearest big hill, brace themselves and face right into it!'

Once clear, Gentry hauled on the brake and dropped down from the seat. He took the shovel from the back and began loading buffalo manure into the wagon.

Tyler watched him quizzically. 'What you doing, kid?'

'We need a bonding agent for the sand. I've heard tell horse manure is good. Don't see why this stuff shouldn't work just as well.'

While Gentry continued with his task, Tyler took the opportunity to build himself a smoke. 'You live and learn.'

NINE

Tyler had been referring to his map with increasing frequency and was yet again poring over it. He surveyed the country around them, noting aspects of flatness that were lost on his companion, checking proportions against his chart. 'Thought so,' he beamed. 'Somewhere over to the west, just over the horizon, lies the Red River and Fargo.'

Not much further on, he pointed to a pile of stones some distance to their left. 'There it is! That's where we put poor old Three-Fingers to rest. We're nearly there. Ain't far now, kid.'

An hour on, he gestured ahead excitedly, slightly to the west. 'There she is – Eldorado!'

Gentry noted some odd shapes on the horizon.

'It was Little Billy spotted it,' Tyler explained. 'He was scouting round for game – we were a mite sick of hardtack and buffalo. You know, up here buffalo tongue is a delicacy – *yuck*. Anyway, he came across it and had a nose around on his ownsome. When he returned, he told us about it but we paid it no never-mind. At the time we were more interested in the geese and prairie chickens he had bagged. That is until Mississippi brought the news from Fargo about the territory crawling with agents on the lookout for us. We had to find somewhere quick. We didn't know the locality or have time to go scouting round. The place Little Billy had stumbled on was the only place we knew of – but if it was as desolate as he had said, it would be ideal.'

'What is it?'

'A ghost town. Yeah, a complete town where folks have just upped sticks and moved on.'

'I've heard tell of such places but never seed one.'

'Ain't surprising,' Tyler said, as they

trundled towards their destination. ‘Moving out from St Jo, then spending all your time in that smithy back in Hicksville, you ain’t seen much of the world at all. Me, I been all over, learned about places. For instance, one thing I’ve learned about the territory up here, it ain’t good for nothing. That’s why it’s littered with deserted towns and farms. You’ve seen some of ’em on the journey up. See, when the first settlers came out here, all they could see was a vast territory covered in green and buffalo – just like Texas, they thought, only a tad colder. You couldn’t blame ’em. The land was dirt cheap. All they had to do was bring in cattle breeds with longer fur, some of them Scottish breeds for instance.’

‘So what’s wrong with the territory?’

‘What the incomers didn’t realize is that the ‘green’ is *prairie weed.* While buffalo thrive on it, cattle need grass. In time their cattle had eaten what little good grass there was. If they didn’t starve they froze to death come the first bad winter. You can’t make a living from farming either. The growing season is short; rainfall's low and unreliable. As with cattle, one bad season and you're wiped out. So it ain't good for a goddamn thing. Except for hiding gold in!'

As the buildings loomed larger, Tyler got more excited. 'The end of the rainbow. The answer to all your dreams, young man.'

'That's if the gold's still there. Don't count your chickens – whether they're Rhode Island Reds or prairie chickens. It's been four, five months now. Anything could have happened. Somebody could have stumbled on it.'

'Don't tempt fate, kid.'

The light was fast disappearing when they finally rode into the ghost town. Long grass swished on the underside of the wagon as they rolled along what had once been the main drag.

'It looks just the same,' Tyler said. 'Figure nothing's been disturbed. That's a good sign.'

They passed neglected, rusted-up machinery, derelict buildings, pitiful remnants of what must have once been a thriving community. Here and there, skeletons of covered wagons that had once been driven by optimistic settlers. Some buildings were leaning at dangerous angles. Others had already collapsed.

'The smithy's at the end,' he explained. 'We may as well use that as our sleeping quarters too.'

They pulled up in the blacksmith's yard which was overgrown with weeds like everywhere else. Gentry hauled on the brake and they dropped down. 'You're more familiar with the place,' he said. 'Know where there's a pump? Have to water the horses, feed 'em and such.'

'More important than horses,' Tyler said, 'let's check the gold's still intact.'

The horses had done a good job and were at the end of a long trail so Gentry disagreed with his companion's priorities but shrugged. 'You're the boss.'

Tyler took an oil-lamp from the wagon and mounted the boardwalk. Gentry followed him, treading carefully along the crumbling walkway. He glanced through doorways as they passed. Very little left of anything. Passers-through would have long taken whatever had any value. Some windows were boarded up as though the folks leaving had some forlorn hope that they might return.

'This is it,' Tyler said, stopping in front of a building with wide doors, indicating that it had once served as a livery stable. He tried the doors but they wouldn't budge. The building had succumbed to the battering winds and was leaning threateningly. Consequently the doorframes were distorted.

'You got bigger muscles than me,' he said. 'You have a go.'

Gentry tugged, heaved and finally got one door slightly ajar.

'Good,' Tyler said, excitedly pushing in front of the other and squeezing into the building.

'Don't think we'll be able to close it again,'

Gentry said, examining the jambs as he followed through.

The interior was cobwebby. On either side: rows of what would have been horse stalls. He cast his eyes over the roof and walls. Old timbers, beams and boards, so rotten they looked likely to fall at any moment. Up one corner, the massed wreckage of broken furniture.

'The magic number three,' Tyler said. 'The third stall. It's in there. Go and fetch the shovel.'

When Gentry returned Tyler had cleared away debris and straw from the stall to expose the hard earth floor.

'Just to the side there,' the older man said, pointing.

'How far down?' Gentry asked as he rammed his foot on the top of the spade.

'Coupla feet.'

After five minutes he hit something hard.

'That'll be it,' Tyler said, hearing the thud. 'Steady does it now.'

Gentry put down his spade and lay down

beside the hole so that he could reach in and scoop out soil with his hands. By the time he had exposed a significant area of flat surface, Tyler had lit the oil-lamp. Gentry spat on his hand to clear away a small area – and in the light of lamp he could make out the yellow gleam of metal.

Gentry had never seen gold before. He ran his fingers over it. Strange. In his line of work he was used to the feel of metal – but this felt inexplicably different from any metal he had ever touched.

Tyler pulled him out of the way. 'Here, you hold the lamp.'

The older man lay down and reached into the pit. In his excitement, he misjudged the weight, and tried to lift an ingot with one hand. He grunted and eased forward so he could use both hands. But even two hands were not enough for the old man given that he was reaching deep and at an awkward angle. He pulled back. 'You get one out,' he said irritatedly, as though he was losing some implicit honour by not being the first to get a grip on it. 'So we can *feel* it.'

Gentry realized the old man's problem. Although he could extract an ingot with more ease, the object was composed of something denser than he had ever handled.

The old man took it. 'Get that chair over there.'

When the chair was in position he dropped onto it and cradled the bar on his legs. It was the first time the oldster had spent any recent period without jabbering. Gentry hunkered beside him, as he wiped it clean.

From his lowly position he could see Tyler's eyes. Something strange had entered them. The man seemed mesmerized by the gold. Gentry had heard of something called gold-fever. Well, if there was such a thing, he reckoned he was seeing it now in his companion's eyes.

After an inordinate length of silence the old man motioned for him to take it. 'Put it back and shove some of the filling back in the hole, just in case.'

When they had strewn some garbage over

it they went to check the smithy.

'Will that do?' Tyler asked when they got there.

Gentry noted the same bits and pieces that characterized the interiors of most of the buildings: chests, barrels and broken-legged furniture. He pushed some stave-sprung kegs out of the way and crossed to the brick furnace. Seemed intact. He ran a finger over the surface. How much dust had been laid down? Five years worth, ten years? He glanced up. Chimney seemed intact too.

'Mr Morse, I reckon we're in business.' He crossed to one of the walls and slipped his flattened palm in between two of the outer planks. 'One thing: if we're going to use the smithy for sleeping in too, we're gonna have to fill these gaps. I ain't been in this acre of God's own country long, but long enough to know how cold the nights can be. And if we don't do something about all these holes the northern Dakota wind is gonna be coming through them like some goddamn express train.'

TEN

After breakfasting Gentry set to checking out the smithy in earnest and preparing it for the job in hand.

'We got to tidy the place up a bit,' he explained. 'We gotta minimize the risk of impurities getting into the molten metal. We're not going to be able to get rid of all the dust but we need it to be as clean as we can get it in the circumstances.'

After a period of brushing and cleaning surfaces he brought tools from the wagon.

'Hell,' he said suddenly, slamming his forehead, 'we ain't got a saw.'

'What do you need a saw for?'

'To make the boxes. I brung wood, hammer, nails. How the hell did I forget a saw?'

'Yeah, how come?'

'I'm a metal worker, Tyler, not a carpenter.

That's how come.'

'Can't we just break the wood to shape. They're only slats.'

Gentry shook his head. 'We're talking about a delicate operation here, Tyler. The two halves have got to be *exact* fits. It's a precision job. Can only be done by careful sawing and that means proper sawing.'

He looked at his companion. 'You know your way around these parts. Where's the nearest settlement.'

'That'll be Fargo.'

'OK, you're familiar with the geography and you're the horseman out of the two of us. Ride back to Fargo and buy us a saw.'

'And leave you here with the gold?' Tyler sneered. 'You think I got half the brain of a flea-bit coyote?'

'We're pardners, ain't we?'

'Not that much of pardners. You go.'

Gentry shrugged. 'As you say. But it'll take longer. I ain't the world's best horseman.'

'You'll manage.'

The words were delivered with hardness

and Gentry eyed his companion. Was it his imagination or had the guy taken on a change since he'd sat in that chair cradling the gold in his hands?

'Yeah, I'll manage,' he rejoined with the same lack of friendliness. 'And while I'm away, you make yourself useful at last and get the furnace going. And look for something small and flat. Preferably metal. I need something for tamping the mixture down hard.'

He walked towards the door, stopping at the wall on his way, and pointed at one of the large cracks still open to the elements. 'And while you're at it, do something about these. Last night, there was so much cold blasting through, if I'd been one of your buffalo, I'd've faced right into one of these.'

He didn't get back till late morning.

'I was hoping to start the casting later this afternoon,' he said glancing at the sun. 'But thanks to that little excursion we've lost a couple of valuable hours, so we won't be able to get round to casting until tomorrow.'

With that he set to making the boxes and by mid-afternoon he was ready for the next stage.

'We'll do one by itself as a test run,' he said. He laid out a double sheet of newspaper by the straw with the instruction for his companion to break the blades up as finely as he could.

Taking one of the pails, he part-filled it with sand. Then he took a handful of buffalo manure and worked it into the material. After a while he poured in some molasses and worked that into the mixture. 'Let's have a look at the straw.'

He took a handful of the crumbled straw and tested its consistency. 'Seems fine enough.' He resumed mixing while slowly sprinkling a handful into the bucket.

'An unholy mess,' Tyler observed, wrinkling his nose.

'This is all to bind the sand,' Gentry explained, judging the texture once more and adding a little more of the molasses.

He poured some of the mixture into one of the boxes. He picked up the iron plate that Tyler had found. He laid the iron plate across the sand and rammed it down with the hunk of timber. Before the box was full he laid the statue in the centre and added sand around it until half the figurine was covered. Then he tamped down the mixture until it was firm and level. He scored two grooves, one from the base, the other at the top.

'That's where we pour the gold in,' he explained, pointing to the bottom one, 'what we call the ingate. And the other, the outgate, is to vent the displaced air.'

He took a sheet of newspaper and, ripping it to shape, laid it across the sand till only the back of the statue was visible 'That's to keep the two mixes separate,' he said.

He repeated the whole process with another box.

'Now this is the tricky bit,' he said. 'It's got to be turned upside down and placed on the first one.'

'Won't the sand drop out?'

'Odds on it will. That's why it's the tricky bit!'

The mixture did come loose and he had to clear the mess away and prepare the top box again.

When it was topped up he considered it before acting.

'I reckon the art is turning it over quicker,' he said. 'Come on, give me a hand.'

The second time the sand in the upper box stayed dutifully in place. He tamped the back of the container so that the rear of the statue would make an impression.

When the two halves were flush he stood back. 'Now we wait for the thing to dry out. With the furnace going in here, it's quite warm so it shouldn't take too long.'

'Shall we start on another in meantimes?'

'No, the mixture needs to be fresh each time otherwise it might be too dry to use when we need it. Once we're sure we've got the technique right, then we can start preparing them one after the other. Might not even need new ones. If we don't damage them we should be able to use the same moulds.'

He went to the door and looked out. 'Nothing we can do now but wait.'

'How long?'

'Dunno, maybe a couple of hours.'

'You don't know how long?'

Gentry smiled humourlessly. 'You seem to be forgetting, I'm new to this game. In a couple of hours I'll test them to see if they've dried out properly.'

'Can't we put them on the furnace? That'd sure dry 'em out quick.'

'Yeah, and crack 'em. Then we'd have to start all over again.'

They left the smithy and took a bite to eat.

'I'll get the pot and make some coffee,' Tyler said as he cut off another chunk of jerky. A minute later he was returning with a coffee pot in one hand – and a saw in the other. 'Look what I found in the wagon. Hell, you didn't forget to bring a saw after all.'

'No.' There was no surprise in Gentry's voice.

'So,' Tyler said impatiently, dropping the implement at the other's feet, 'did you forget *that* you'd brung it?'

'No,' the other said, enigmatically leaving the word hanging in the air.

'Well?'

'See,' Gentry went on to explain, 'you tell me you're no half-brained coyote. Well, I'll let you in on a little secret – neither am I.' He nodded back to the smithy. 'When we've finished our little job in there, you'll have no need of my services or me. Who knows what you might do? I got a feeling there might be a whole new side to you that I don't know about. Maybe a hard side that you didn't show when we first met.'

'Hell, no. I wouldn't do anything like that. We're pals, Gentry.'

'Well, when that thought occurred to me,' the younger man continued, 'I figured now was the time to do something about covering myself. I needed an excuse to go to Fargo –

and while I was there I dropped off a little letter. To who doesn't concern you, but it tells the receiver to open it if I don't get back in a specified time. It names you, describes you in great detail. Explains all about the gold-heist and our operation here. All about the statues and what your plans are. The upshot is, you put me out of the way and you'll have civilian law and army investigators – both here and up in Canada – on the lookout for you. And with your putting me away, they'll want you for murder too!'

Tyler's face was black. 'Thought we were pardners.'

'Like you said a while back: not that much of pardners. I just feel safer with some insurance.'

'Some smart kid.'

'Oh, I don't know about that. Let's just say, I ain't the durndest of fools. On the other hand, if I get back safe and sound, the letter won't be opened and no one will be any the wiser.' He nodded back at the wagon. 'Now if you'll get the coffee and mugs, we'll have those drinks you were talking about.'

A couple of hours on, they returned to the smithy and separated the two halves.

'Not exactly perfect,' Gentry said when he had extracted the statue and examined the impressions. 'But it'll do.'

He mixed a container of whitewash and applied it to the surfaces. 'Now all we have to do is wait for that to dry and we're in business.'

When he finally checked them, they were OK but it was near midnight.

'I'm bushed, 'he said. 'Next shift – the casting – starts at dawn. We'll leave the furnace going. Save us a job in the morning.'

ELEVEN

Given the cold northern Dakota nights, keeping the furnace going permanently served to keep them warm while sleeping in the smithy. They agreed it was incumbent upon whoever felt the need to get up to relieve themselves during the night that they should throw some more fuel through the furnace door.

After breakfast, Gentry slapped his hands. 'OK, time for the yellow stuff.'

They unearthed a couple of ingots and brought them to the smithy.

'Figure it will take between one and half to two ingots for each statue,' he said as he cleaned them down. In the cold light of day, the radiance of the metal was duller. Its appearance was more ordinary. Was this the thing that men had sought and killed for since the beginning of time? he pondered as he hefted one in his hand. One by one he dropped them on their ends into the ladle.

'OK,' he said, 'open the door with the tongs.'

Having two ingots in the ladle with its long handle, it took all his strength to insert the lot into the furnace.

In time inspection showed the metal to be bubbling.

'Like I've told you,' Gentry said, 'gold ain't my speciality and these ain't perfect conditions. I reckon the temperature's not as high as it should be, so we have to act quick. We'll put the mould as close to the furnace door as we can. And you open it smart when I say so. And keep clear if you want to keep your arms and legs.'

He needn't have worried. Although this was not *his* craft, he was a craftsman and the operation went without a hitch.

After it had cooled he separated the two halves and beamed in satisfaction. Tyler made to touch the effigy.

‘Oh, no,’ Gentry said, pulling his hand away. ‘It’s set but it ain’t that cool.’ He smiled and looked at his companion. ‘You just can’t keep your hands off the stuff, can you?’

Tyler looked sheepish. ‘Yeah, kinda gets you, don’t it?’

‘Well, as you like to do all the touching,’ Gentry said, ‘you can have the job of buffing.’

‘What’s that?’

‘See all those rough bits and surfaces? They need smoothing. That’s your job.’

After lunch the cast statue was still warm but cool enough to be taken out of the mould. They laid it on a makeshift bench and when it had been buffed it presented a reasonable facsimile.

‘Gonna be a sacrilege covering such a thing of beauty in store-bought paint,’ Tyler mused.

Gentry grunted. ‘Wrong choice of word there, pal. Sacrilege is what we did in stealing the original from the church, not to mention the unholy way we're using the Holy Virgin.'

Tyler was mesmerized again by the look of the metal and didn't hear.

'Anyways,' Gentry went on, 'with regard to more technical matters, it needs to be quite cold when you paint it. Otherwise the paint will crack. So we'll stand it outside now. In fact, as the statues are gonna be travelling in back of a cold wagon, we'll keep 'em all outside once they've been painted so they're not subject to unnecessary temperature change. And, just in case, put on several layers of plain undercoat before you start with the pretty colours.'

'We might as well bring the other ingots over,' Tyler said when they'd taken the first figurine outside. 'Now that we know the method's working we can stack them all in the smithy.'

Shortly they had moved most of the ingots.

'There's something else in here,' Gentry said as he raised the last bar from the hole.

'Packets of some kind.'

'Oh, yeah,' Tyler said, peering in. 'I'd forgot about them. Leave 'em be. It's old Confederate money. It was worth something when we first took it, but now it's useless. All Reb money has officially been declared void as the product of an illegal regime. All they're good for now is keeping the furnace going!'

'How much is there?'

'Don't know. We never bothered to count it. A hundred thousand – who knows? – maybe more. And all useless. Huh, the fortunes of war.'

'From what you say,' Gentry observed, 'more like the *mis*fortune of war.'

'Yeah, come on let's get back to work.'

Three days on they were moving to completion. Gentry had been almost right in his calculations. It was working out that the sixteen ingots were providing the material for twelve statutes.

Eight were already painted and boxed.

Three were being painted and there was enough metal in the furnace for maybe one more.

Gentry had just closed the door after checking the state of the metal in the ladle when Tyler put down his paintbrush. He crossed to the blacksmith and put his hand on his arm. 'Listen.'

'What's the matter?'

Tyler put his finger to his lips. 'Quiet. I think I heard something outside.'

Gentry chuckled. 'It's just the wind. I been hearing the creaks of old wood all over the place ever since we came here.'

'This sounded different.'

'It's your imagination,' Gentry said, and continued with his task.

A minute later, Tyler repeated the action of putting his fingers to his lips. 'There it is again,' he whispered, taking out his gun. 'That ain't no wind – or my imagination. Sounds like somebody's out front.'

'Your Copperhead maybe?' Gentry questioned, going to the stack of his personal belongings and taking out the Navy Colt.

'No. Don't think he's got the brains to follow me up here. Besides, he's got so little control of his temper he would have come blasting straight in. You carry on like nothing's wrong. I'm going outside to investigate.'

Gentry looked at the gun in his hand. So concerned had he been with other matters during the journey that he still hadn't undertaken any practice with the gun. But he checked the thing was loaded; he knew that much. He placed it close at hand and resumed his work while the other went to the back door and opened it as quietly as he could.

The smith had just poured another ladle of gold into a mould when the front door crashed open. He whirled round to see Tyler manhandling a woman into the building.

Even in the poor shadowy light of the oil-lamps he could see she was young and had a certain prettiness. Judging by her buckskin-clad legs he reckoned that under the thick fur-collared jacket she had a slender frame.

'Look what we got here,' Tyler said, pushing the girl forward. 'Got a hoss and a fully provisioned mule in tow.' He pulled off her fur cap so that long, black hair fell into her turned-up collar.

'Why did you bring her in here?' Gentry asked, putting down the ladle. 'Now she's seen what we're doing.'

'She knows,' Tyler snapped. 'Caught her snooping round the front, looking through the cracks. I've checked. We never filled in all of 'em. Some of 'em we left are as big as a frigging window. She'd seen enough already.' Keeping his gun on her, he grabbed the back of a chair and thrust it forward. 'Put your keester on that, missy, and tell us what you're doing out here.'

She sat down. 'I saw the smoke from the chimney. Wondered what was going on.'

'That's a thin story, missy. Don't explain what you're doing out in this god-forsaken wilderness in the first place.'

'I was just riding through.'

'This ain't the kind of place you ride

through. It's on the road from nowhere to nowhere. Come on, spit it out. What you doing here?'

'I've told you. There's nothing else to say.'

Tyler eyed her, then slapped her face with his free hand.

Gentry dashed forward and interposed himself between Tyler and the girl. 'No call for that,' he said, pushing the older man back a step. 'We don't hit women where I come from.'

Tyler jabbed the gun in Gentry's midriff. 'Whether you like it or not, we're playing for high stakes here, son. And we're in it together. And we gotta find out what this doll's up to. Now out of my way.'

Gentry hesitated, staring hard into the other's eyes. 'OK. I'm as intrigued as you are about what this gal's doing here, but no more rough stuff.' With that he stepped slowly aside.

'Right,' Tyler continued, looking back at the girl. 'Now we got that out of the way, let's start again. There's more to this than you just riding through. We ain't jackasses, missy.' His tone became even harder. 'Despite what the big fellow says, this is the kind of place where a nosy female can disappear with nobody the wiser. So, come on, lady, what's it all about?'

She looked at Gentry as though in anticipation of him interceding again, but his eyes gave nothing away. 'I've already explained,' she said falteringly.

'You've explained nothing,' Tyler pressed. 'You know why I'm suspicious? You got a Southern manner of speech. And I think, what's a Southern belle doing this far north – out in the wilds of northern Dakota Territory?'

'Yes, I am from the South,' she said. 'And proud of it.'

'Go on.'

She paused and when she resumed, there was a new forthrightness in her voice. 'My name is Beatrice Fayette, Mr Morse.'

Tyler's mouth tightened and he looked at Gentry. 'See, she knows my name. I told you there was more to this.' He turned back to the girl. 'So, how come you know my name?

'More important than my name,' she said, 'or yours – is that of my husband. Major Fayette, late of the Confederacy. Does that name mean anything to you?'

'No. Should it?'

'My husband was the officer in charge of a unit trying to get to the border with a very important shipment.'

Tyler nodded. 'I might be beginning to understand. Would this be at the end of the war?'

'That's right. The unit came under heavy fire and my father and all his men were killed. Following the fighting the shipment disappeared. Many officers and agents were put on the job but came up with nothing. There were many rumours. One that it found its way into Mexico and then was spirited away. I didn't hold with that because that was the obvious route and it was heavily covered by investigating officers.'

Content with nodding, the two men remained silent now that the girl was talking at last.

'No,' she continued, 'the one notion that I think had the most credence was that the shipment was taken by civilians who then headed north with the hope of getting it to Canada. Now nothing has been heard and there have been no reports of gold bars of any quantity turning up.'

'This is very absorbing, Miss Fayette,' Tyler said, 'but what is your interest? After all, from what you say, it was all some time ago.'

'My family had a small plantation. In the final stages of the conflict our place was razed to the ground during which action my father was killed. Our workers were driven off, our slaves freed. Then my mother died – her death, I firmly believe, hastened by the disasters I have just described. The upshot was, Mr Morse, that when my husband was also killed right at the end of the war I was left completely alone. I had, indeed, *have* nothing to my name.

'What could I do? I have no useful education. I was raised in dining-rooms and parlours, and taught nothing more useful than polite conversation, needlepoint, embroidery and such. There was nothing for it but for me to go into service. I, who was used to being waited upon all my life. I would countenance such employment, but only after I had exhausted all other avenues. I pondered upon my circumstance, asking what did I know that would have a premium in what Mr Thackeray called Vanity Fair?'

For the first time a faint smile came to her face, as she noted Tyler's puzzled expression. 'The term refers to the Business of Life, Mr Morse. Then I realized my advantages. I knew there was a gold shipment hidden somewhere. If I could locate it, I would be the recipient of some reward that would help me overcome my penury.'

'That's one hell of an operation for a mere girl to contemplate,' Tyler put in.

'Although a mere girl, I had some advantages. I was raised among horses and could ride almost before I could walk. Therefore I could ride with some skill. Moreover, coming from a military family and being surrounded by military personnel who talked openly in front of a woolly-headed girl, I knew many details. Further, I could visit likely places where information might be forthcoming and I, as a mere girl, would not be suspected – which gave me an edge over heavy-footed investigators. I learned your name and the names of the other men who had taken advantage of the nest-egg which had fallen into their lap. Also, week by week, investigators have been taken off the case so that there are few remaining. Leaving the field more open to me – a mere girl.'

'Gee,' Tyler commented. 'You have been a busy girl.'

'Unfortunately, whenever I got a lead to one of the gang, I discovered he had been killed. By my reckoning there are only two left now: you and a man known as Copperhead. I was on the trail of this Copperhead fellow when, by chance, I was passing through Gage City and learned of you and Mr Jones becoming acquainted. Although you left town at different times, I put two and two together and hazarded the guess that you might be rendezvousing. When Mr Jones left a few days on, I trailed his wagon and found, when I got to Bailey's Halt, that my guess had been right.'

A vitality was now strong in her eye. 'Does that explain my presence here?'

Tyler nodded. 'I'm impressed, ma'am.' He let the information sink in, then said, 'But, if we were to set you free, what would you be aiming to do, now you've found us and the gold? Go and tell the authorities to claim the reward?'

'Not only am *I* impressed,' Gentry butted in before she had a chance to reply, 'but I reckon Mrs Fayette has as much claim on the gold as we do. Given the fact it has her husband's blood on it, *more* right in fact.'

Tyler sniffed dismissively, keeping his eyes on the woman but nodding in Gentry's direction. 'That's the honest blacksmith talking,' he explained in a cynical tone. He pondered on it. 'Now, the notion of setting you free and letting you go to the law don't sit well with me one bitty little bit. But there is something in what my friend says.' He thought more on it. 'Looking at it from your point of view, a third cut would be a sight bigger than a measly reward.' He looked at Gentry. 'On the condition she don't go blabbing, what do you say to us cutting her in on a third?'

'I figure that's fair and proper.'

'I thought you'd say something like that,' Tyler said. 'And you, ma'am? You're agreeable to such an arrangement?'

'Yes.'

Tyler leant forward and shook her hand. 'OK, ma'am, it's a deal. And real sorry about that slap.'

'You are a gentleman after all,' Gentry said.

'Don't know about that,' Tyler said, 'but what I do know: now she's said yes, she's as involved as we are, so it ain't going to be in her interests to spill the beans to no law officers!'

'OK,' Gentry added, 'if not a gentleman, then a wily old coot. Method in madness.' He smiled at the girl. 'You like some coffee, ma'am? After all that, I think we could do with some.' He walked to the stove and nodded to the array of brushes and coloured pots on the table. 'By the way, you any good at painting? My artistic friend here has painted eight Madonnas so far – and I have yet to see one that even resembles a woman!'

TWELVE

It took them one more day. The girl proved herself to be a useful addition to the group. Not only did she prove to be quite adept at painting, but food from her provisions added a welcome variety to their limited and increasingly boring diet.

During the last evening they discussed the roles they would play if challenged on the final lap of their journey north. As already planned, they were to be priests, and it was deemed that the new member of their team would be passed off as a church helper. Over coffee they pooled their scant knowledge of religious matters, developed some patter and rehearsed their lines.

Then the two men tried on their black suits. They were acceptable fits.

'What do priests wear round their necks?'

Tyler said, pointing to his bare throat. 'This don't look right.'

'I think they wear some kind of special collar,' Gentry said.

The older man grunted. 'Well, that's something we've overlooked.'

Beatrice, who had been sitting on a stool, watching the parade, stood up. 'I might be able to do something about that,' she said. Rummaging through her belongings, she pulled out a silk petticoat. She cut a couple of strips. One by one, she tied them round the necks of the two men, pinning the items fussily into shape, and then stood back to admire her work.

'I think those have the right dignity,' she said. 'The only problem is you're looking more like Quakers.'

'That's OK,' Tyler said. 'We'll be Quakers.'

'No, no,' she chided. 'Quakers don't hold with religious artefacts. They wouldn't be hauling Madonna statues.'

'Then what do we say we are?' Gentry asked.

'I'll think of something,' she said. 'But whatever I come up with, let's hope if anybody stops us they aren't too knowledgeable with regard to religious sects.'

In the morning Gentry heated up water on the furnace and filled a tub so they would have some appearance of cleanliness in keeping with their roles as priests. The two men kept dutifully out of the way while Beatrice bathed first.

When it was time to leave, the two men donned the dark suits and Beatrice fixed the special collars in place.

'My,' she said when, after attending to Gentry's neckwear, she stroked his newly-shaven cheek. 'Who would have known there was a handsome man under all that stubble.'

'Right,' Tyler said when they were outside and packaged to go, 'it will be more fitting for Beatrice to ride in the wagon with you, Gentry. I'll take one of the horses.'

He headed the procession out, shouting back, 'From now on, we avoid all settlements. We either bivouac in a sheltered spot on the plains or, with a bit of luck, we might run across another derelict town. There's enough of them up here.'

But as the day wore on, it got colder and, not coming across any abandoned property, they were reconciling themselves to a night on the plains. The problem with that was, they had ditched the hides that they had used as cover for the earlier stage of their journey. Luckily they came across some travelling Lakota. Even luckier, the Indians had some hides and blankets which they were willing to sell; so the trio's night under the stars was not as bad as it could have been.

The following day the weather brightened. They progressed in hope that the weather wouldn't demonstrate one of its capricious swings. There was no incident until Gentry suddenly shouted, 'There's two riders ahead.'

Tyler drew level with the driving seat and squinted. 'Your eyes are better than mine, younker. Can't see nobody.'

'Yes,' Beatrice confirmed. 'Two. On the skyline.'

'Which way they headed?' Tyler wanted to know.

'This a-way.'

Some seconds on, Tyler said, 'Yeah, I can see 'em now. What's that flashing?'

'Looks like sun glinting off badges, old-timer,' Gentry said. 'Gotta be the law. Reckon this is where we find out if your disguises work.'

They were eventually requested to stop by raised hands from the strangers. Gentry complied and the two riders nudged their animals closer.

'State your names and business,' a man with a marshal's badge ordered.

'I am Father Travis,' Tyler said, summoning up a slow, precise tone of speaking, 'and this is Father Carrington.'

'And the young lady?'

'Joan, my dear cousin,' Tyler explained. 'She helps on church matters. She is indispensable with the paperwork.'

'And what's your business out here in the sticks?'

'Delivering Our Lady to various missions.'

'What the hell does that mean?' the other asked. The questioner was younger and wore a deputy's badge.

'Fred,' his superior snapped. 'Watch your language in front of these good people. And before a female too. Sorry, folks, like all youngsters today, he's a mite short on etiquette.'

Beatrice gestured to the back of the wagon. 'We have been entrusted with the transportation of figurines of Our Lady to outlying missions,' she said in the clipped tones associated with the East Coast. 'Even out here in the sticks, as you refer to it, young man, reminders of the omnipresence of our Our Lord and Holy Mother are necessary.'

'Then you're Roman,' the deputy put in.

'That is correct, my son,' Tyler said.

The deputy looked askance. 'Well, all the Catholic priests I ever seen have wore a monk's habit and rope sandals,' he said stiffly.

'That is quite likely, my son,' Tyler said. 'But we are Jesuits. Our order allows us to wear contemporary clothes when we are out in the general community.' He pointed to his neck. 'Save for the distinguishing symbol of our collars, of course.'

The young lawman did not look convinced. 'And why are priests doing the menial work of delivering?' he pressed. 'The statues could be delivered by regular freight workers.'

'The Holy Father has decreed that the delivery of such icons can only be entrusted to the ordained,' Beatrice put in. 'Besides, the fathers conduct an official service of blessing after each installation.'

'Seems all square to me,' the marshal said.

'I still wanna check the load,' his deputy insisted.

'Is that all right with you, Father?' the marshal asked. 'My young colleague is a tad eager in the pursuance of his responsibilities. See, fact is, we been briefed to look out for a gang heisting gold who might be heading this way.'

'I understand,' Tyler said. 'No need to explain.' He gestured to the load. 'Be my guest.'

The deputy nudged his horse to the wagon and clambered over the side. He untied the knots and threw back the tarp. 'These look well fixed down. You got some tool for prising them open?'

'I am afraid not, my son' Tyler said.

The man stood erect and opened his jacket to draw a huge hunting knife from a sheath round his waist. It took him a minute to work one of the lids loose. He removed the top layer of straw and examined the uncovered statue. Then he felt around the rest of the straw in the box. He grunted and returned the contents to their original condition and tapped the lid in place with the butt of his knife.

'Now are you satisfied, Fred?' the marshal asked.

'No. I want to see one from underneath.

Mind giving me a hand, chief?'

The other reluctantly joined him and the two officers stacked a couple of boxes on the side to give them access to a bottom one.

'Jeez, these are heavy,' the deputy said.

'What have I told you about your language,' the other snapped.

'I agree they are heavy,' Beatrice put in. 'Marble is not the lightest of materials.'

'Marble?' the deputy queried as he tackled the second box.

'Yes,' Beatrice said. 'Extracted from the quarries near Rome itself.'

The young man opened the new lid. 'It's the first time I've seen marble painted.'

'It's a venerable tradition,' Beatrice explained. 'Indeed, the great Michelangelo was known to paint some of his marble statues.'

'Well, I hope he could paint better than this,' the keen youngster muttered under his breath as he completed his inspection.

'Feel free to examine others,' Tyler said.

'No,' the marshal said, throwing a stern look at his underling, 'we've seen ample and we've troubled you good people enough. And thank you for bearing with us.'

'We have our job to do, my son,' said Tyler, 'and so do you.'

The officers replaced the tarp and mounted up. 'Again, sorry to have troubled you, Father,' the lawman said. He tipped his hat to Beatrice with a 'ma'am' and the two galloped away.

'Well, it worked,' Tyler said when they were out of earshot. 'Now, let's get moving.'

Gentry flicked the ribbons and smiled. 'By Jimmy, even I would have believed Beatrice here. Where did you learn to talk in that cut-glass way?'

'We have relatives out in New England and we visited regularly in my younger years. To their consternation, I used to enjoy mimicking my cousins.'

'And where did you learn the ten-dollar words?'

'I have already told you, Mr Jones, I was raised in the parlours of Southern gentlefolk.'

THIRTEEN

Late in the afternoon they spotted a small clutch of buildings to the west. Tyler rode out to investigate, returning to inform them it was an abandoned farm. 'May as well take advantage of it,' he said. 'Can't rely on coming across anything as good before sundown.'

Gentry swung the wagon in its direction and soon they were passing broken, drunken fences that had once marked out corrals and holding-pens.

But after their night on the plains it was like living in luxury. The buildings weren't quite as dilapidated as the ghost town. There was more intact furniture and a usable stable for the animals. They chose one of the farmhouses as the base for their stay and Gentry toured the place looking for anything useful. He returned minutes later with a couple of rusting oil-lamps in one hand and a couple of mattresses tucked under his other arm. He dropped the latter on the floor, then noted Beatrice's turned up nose.

'Don't worry about bedbugs, ma'am,' he grinned. 'In this climate the little buggers will have frozen to death by now.'

'Do we toss a coin for them?' Tyler asked.

'No,' Gentry said. 'The lady naturally shall have one and I reckon your ancient bones justify you having the other. I'll find something. A bigger problem is water. I didn't see no rivers or streams as we rode in so I figure this place must have had its own water supply somewhere. I'll see what I can turn up.'

Eventually he found a pump behind one of the buildings. At first it clanked noisily, loose and dry. But in time he felt some resistance, sensing that far below it was beginning to get a grip of something. He repeated the levering until the action began to take a toll on his muscles and a brown sludge began to drip from the nozzle. In time the gunge thinned. It seemed an eternity before the liquid took on the appearance of water. He put a drop to his lips. Seemed like the real stuff. To be on the safe side he clanked some more. He scouted around the buildings until he found a container.

With water they now lacked nothing and, to celebrate their good fortune, Beatrice cooked an especially resplendent meal. After coffee Gentry went to tend to the animals. After he had fed and watered them, Beatrice joined him to help in rubbing them down.

'What are you going to do with your share?' she asked.

'I never count my chickens,' he said. 'Besides this escapade is a whole new thing for me.' He rubbed his arms. 'Let's get back to the fire. It's cold in here.'

'No. Let's talk awhile.'

'What is there to talk about?'

She found an upended stool, righted it and sat down. 'Well, for a start, you know all about my involvement in this business. I've come clean, as I believe is the parlance. But how did you get into it?'

He leaned against a stanchion, and slowly related the circumstances. It was the first time he had really talked about his wife and what had happened to her; and she sensed the emotion in his voice.

He paused and took time in building a cigarette and lighting it in an attempt to disguise the lump in his throat. When he finished his tale he dropped the butt. As he was twisting it into the ground with his foot, she crossed over to him and she put her arms around him. 'You've been through a deal, Gentry.'

They stayed that way for some time. But he felt gauche and when he could take the awkwardness no longer, he slowly extricated himself from the embrace and crossed the space to sit on the vacated stool. 'OK, young lady,' he said with an embarrassed cough. 'Your turn to tell me more about yourself.'

They talked for some time until Gentry

said, 'Now it *is* time to get back. Old Tyler is going to be feeling lonely.'

'There's something I don't like about that man,' she said.

Gentry chuckled. 'I don't blame him for being jumpy. As you know, there's this Copperhead guy out to kill him. I think I'd be edgy and a mite short of temper if I had to keep looking over my shoulder. But it looks like he's now well clear of the fellow. Other than that, he's just an old buzzard who's getting cantankerous in his old age.' He chuckled again. 'A real weird look came over his face when he first saw the gold. You ought to have seen him. Reckon he had a touch of gold fever for a spell. But it didn't last long. He's over it now.'

He motioned to the door and extended his arm. 'Let me escort you to your quarters, ma'am.'

Silently they crossed the yard, huddled together against the wind and lightly falling snow, watched only by the stars.

'Where have you two been?' Tyler said as

they entered the farmhouse.

'Just girl and boy talk, old-timer,' Gentry grinned. 'Don't worry. We haven't been conspiring. We're not ganging up on you, or aiming to do you out of your share.'

Tyler scowled. 'That ain't a joking matter, son. You don't know what it's like to see all your pardners getting knocked off, and not being able to do anything about it. And knowing you're next in line.'

Gentry yawned and stacked some layers of buffalo-hides on the floor.

'That's right,' Tyler said. 'Time for shut-eye and about time too. We got an early start tomorrow.'

They took up their respective places and bedded down. With lamps turned out and the fire glowing in the stove, Gentry was aware of the faint wind cutting across the plain, rattling the clapboards.

And a little later he was aware of a shape snuggling under the blankets with him. He just hoped it wasn't the old man.

The smell of coffee pervaded his nostrils as he woke. He opened his eyes to see Beatrice at the stove and Tyler seated on his mattress poring over his map. 'Two days at the most and we're over the border,' the old man said.

Gentry rose, crossed to Beatrice and kissed the back of her neck, whispering, 'You know, that's the first night I ain't had a nightmare since I don't remember when.' She nuzzled him and returned to her task.

Tyler didn't hear the words but he saw the action. 'Then I'll be safe,' he said, looking back at his map, 'and we can divvy up the statues – and you two can...' He waved a hand in the air as he sought words, 'You two ... can ... can do whatever you want. So get yourself moving, younker.'

As he sipped his coffee, Gentry watched Beatrice going about her business. At first he had experienced guilt at the feelings that were rising in him for the girl that he had known for such a short period of time, and he had tried to quash them. But the more he thought about it, the more he was beginning to realize that Beatrice was not taking Marybelle's place. She couldn't. No, he shouldn't see it that way. She was a different woman in what was now a different phase of his life. His mind mulled things over. If ever they came through this thing as planned ... if everything went OK...

Outside the place was shrouded in a light fall of snow. They made their various preparations. Beatrice loaded her mule. Gentry tended to the horses while Tyler saw to the loading of the wagon.

Gentry brought out the horses, harnessed them to the wagon and had just gone into the barn to check he hadn't left any tack when he heard a male voice. And it didn't belong to Tyler!

He stepped outside and then heard clearly: 'Going somewhere, Tyler?'

Further up the street was a big man with blond flowing hair. And a rifle held at the hip. Gentry's blood froze. With hair like that, it had to be Copperhead!

Tyler was standing near the wagon, Beatrice by the mule.

Gentry was stymied. Neither he nor Tyler would have any guns. Their weapons were in the back of the wagon. To maintain their disguise they had decided they couldn't travel armed.

'Didn't you hear me, Tyler?' the man boomed. 'I said – you going somewhere?'

'Can't deny that.'

'Never pegged you as a double-crosser. But you know how slow I am.'

Tyler shrugged.

'You are double-crossing, ain't you?"

Tyler thought about it – he had to be careful about his words – then pointed at the wagon. 'You've tracked me up here, Copper. There's the gold. I guess it would be an insult to the intelligence – of even somebody like you – if I tried to deny it.'

'You know when I twigged it was you? When I rode into Jacksburg and got throwed in the slammer charged with murdering Denver.'

Tyler threw a glance at Gentry – as though checking to see whether he was in earshot – then made a step towards the wagon.

The gun barked and dirt flew up at Tyler's feet.

'Don't move!' Copperhead roared, jacking in a new load. 'The next one takes your head off. Like I was saying, they had this very detailed description of me. My hair, the rattler in my hatband, everything.'

'You don't know what you're saying,' Tyler shouted. 'You've gone loco.'

Copperhead ignored him. 'Who gave you this description? I asked them. Wasn't an old guy with a limp? Looks like he wouldn't hurt a fly? Yeah, they said. Well, that's when I tumbled to what was going on.'

'So how did you get out of the slammer?'

Copperhead smiled. 'Well, there was one thing you didn't know. This bad head of mine had given me one my danged tempers and it just happened that I'd smashed a few jaws in a saloon shindig. So at the time I was supposed to be in Jacksburg blasting the life out of poor Denver, I'd spent the night cooling off – courtesy of the local lawman – in a town *fifty* miles from Jacksburg. Lady Luck doesn't often cast her favours my way but she was looking down on me then. She gave me a good lawyer who followed up my story and the murder case was thrown out of court. You know I'm a mite slow in the brain department but even I could figure – if the gang was getting knocked off, and there was finally only two left – me and you – and I knew it wasn't me ... well. Yeah, I have difficulty doing my sums, Tyler, but I could do *that* one.'

Something seemed to give in Tyler. As though it didn't matter who was listening anymore. A veneer dropped and when he spoke his voice was different. 'OK, you got me. It was me. Now all the cards are on the deck. You can see 'em, no cards hidden.'

He tapped the wagon-side. 'We got the gold now, here on the wagon. There's four of us. Come on, Copper. We're all pardners.'

'When it comes to gold, there ain't no

such thing as pardners, Tyler. You've taught me that.'

'Four,' Tyler went on. 'That's a quarter each. You'd be happy with your quarter, wouldn't you?'

'You don't seem to understand. Whatever happens to the gold ain't important right now.'

'No? What's more important?'

Copperhead resumed his walk towards him. 'Blowing your frigging head off, that's what.'

'What? You'd shoot an unarmed man?'

'Tyler, I've never knowed you being unarmed,' Copperhead said, maintaining his advance.

'Yeah, I'm unarmed,' the other said. 'All part of the disguise. See, we're supposed to be priests. Look.' He gestured to his clothing, then raised his arms so that his jacket opened to show that he had no gunbelt. 'That's how we're getting the gold out. In the guise of priests. That's the plan. It's been recast as statues. So we got a clear run into

Canada. Ain't much more than fifty miles to go now.'

'Blab, blab, blab,' Copperhead sneered, waggling his head so that the snake-bones in his hatband rattled. 'I know you. You think you can talk your way out of this one. Well, this time it ain't gonna work. It's just the two of us – and one gun. *This* one.'

Tyler seemed unfazed by the advancing muzzle, now getting threateningly within good shooting range. He nodded to the blacksmith. 'Gentry there, he did the casting. He knows about metal and stuff. These statues, they're that good, they've already passed the scrutiny of one set of lawmen who came a-snooping. You ought to see them, Copper. Here, I'll show you one.'

His arm dipped inside the wagon. 'You can judge for yourself.'

Then, in one movement, he grabbed the hidden rifle and dove forward to the ground.

Copperhead's first bullet splintered the wagon-side. But his second headed for the clouds as he rocketed back from the heavy missile embedded in his chest. His third shot, fired from a hand flat against the dirt, slammed harmlessly into the sidewalk.

Tyler stepped forward, blasting again and the prone figure juddered. He made another step but he needed to go no further to check. His challenger was dead.

'You!' Gentry shouted. 'It was you all along!'

Tyler whirled round as the big smith lumbered towards him. Again he triggered the rifle and Gentry keeled over. Blood streaming from his side, he struggled to his knees.

'Yeah,' Tyler sneered, 'I ain't denying anything.' Copperhead had broadcast the story for all to hear. Gentry had heard the details. But both Copperhead and the blacksmith had bullets in them – there was no more need for subterfuge. 'No point in denying anything.'

'I figure you...' Gentry stuttered, pain contorting his face, 'you ... burnt the smithy ... just to get me ... to do the job.'

'Who else?' Tyler said. There was more

than a hint of pride in his voice. 'I admit to that too, you jughead. I could see that you were a stick-in-the-mud goody-goody, and wouldn't do what I wanted unless everything you had was wiped out.'

He moved towards the downed man. 'The building went up quicker than I intended. Sorry about that, pal. Believe me, I didn't intend what happened to your missus. But the way it turned out it was even better. Her getting burned up helped my cause in making you even more desperate.'

Gentry groped ineffectively at him as he approached.

'But,' Tyler said coldly, 'as my old Italian grandma used to say – *che sera, sera*. What will be will be.' With that he swung the rifle in an arc, smashing the butt against Gentry's head. And the big man thudded into the dirt.

Beatrice screamed and ran over, kneeling by the lifeless figure. She whirled round. 'You conniving, cowardly rat,' she snarled. 'You gonna kill me too? You might as well.

Wipe the board clean.'

'Thanks for the invitation,' Tyler said. 'But, you see, missy, I got *some* scruples. I don't kill unnecessarily. You came muscling in where you weren't wanted, but you ain't no threat no more. You ain't armed and by the time you get to squawk – that's if you ever get out of here – I'll be long gone. With or without your help, the authorities will figure out what's been going on. They ain't stupid. They'll figure that I'm headed for Canada. But by then it'll be too late.'

Without warning, he thrust the rifle butt forward smashing against the side of her head so that she too collapsed. He looked down at her still form alongside that of the smith. 'On the other hand, neither do I believe in tempting fate.'

Without another glance at the scene of mayhem around him he clambered onto the driving-seat of the wagon. He flicked the ribbons and the wagon rolled along the desolate track. At the end he swung left to head north across the rolling plains.

FOURTEEN

'The boys were right,' the man with the star said when he slung open the door of the abandoned smithy.

The first signs had been outside where the lawmen had seen fresh horse droppings. Now, in the smithy there were newly cut remnants of wood on the floor with fresh sawdust; and straw strewn all over the place. Marshal Fullerton sniffed, his nose guiding him eventually to a pail of manure, beside it a pail of molasses. He looked quizzically at them. 'God knows what these are all about, but they must mean something.'

He crossed to the furnace and felt it. 'And this is still warm.'

Meanwhile something caught the eye of his comrade, something glistening in the shaft of sunlight from the open door. The man knelt down. A small ball of shiny metal. He picked it up, rolled it in his hand and took it to his chief. 'Yes, sir, the boys were right after all about the stuff being brought north.'

A detective from a private agency out of Chicago had been following up a long shot. Stuck with no clues, as a last resort he had been tracking a mysterious lone wagon heading north. At that point neither he or his headquarters had any suspicions other than it looked a bit odd. But when the fellow didn't report back to Chicago his boss notified the Dakota Territory headquarters and they sent out their own investigators – who found the private detective gut-shot.

That had been enough to set wheels in motion and a territory-wide alert was organized. Whether or not this wagon had anything to do with the missing gold, its occupants were certainly up to something villainous – and were now wanted on suspicion of murder.

'You know what they done?' Marshal

Fullerton mooted, having confirmed the globule in his hand was a small sample of gold. 'They've melted the stuff down into a different shape. But what?'

Before they left, Tyler and Gentry had had the sense to smash up all the moulds and boxes. Similarly they'd smashed the plaster original and dumped it under the rubble of a collapsed building along with the paints and brushes.

'Come on,' the marshal said, 'let's see if we can find any sign of which way they went.'

Examination of the surrounding ground soon revealed new tracks heading north.

'That's it,' he said. 'They're definitely heading for Canada.' He looked up and down the weed-fringed street. 'Before we go, I wanna know if they brought the gold here to smelt it, or if it was *already* here. Let's have a look-see while we're out here.'

They scouted all the buildings top to bottom, giving especial scrutiny to the floors but found only long-discarded paraphernalia under thick, undisturbed dust. It was clear nothing elsewhere had been touched. Then they circled the adjacent area within a radius of a hundred yards. The ground was as hard as iron, with no signs of recent digging.

'Yeah, they brought the stuff *in*,' he concluded. 'The attraction of this place was the smithy. That's why they came here. Just right for what they wanted – the right facilities out in the middle of nowhere where nobody could see what they were up to. But as for where they stashed the loot for the last six months, this place is a dead end and we may as well forget it. It was hid someplace else.'

He sat down on the boardwalk and built a smoke while he thought on their next move. Behind him was a collapsed livery stable. Flattened to the ground by the wind like much of the rest of town, it was of no interest to him and so they hadn't examined it. What he didn't realize was, it was last night's wind that had finally reduced it to a wreck – and that somewhere under the rubble was a newly dug hole.

He lit his smoke. 'We may as well cross

this place off the map. They just used it for the last stage of their operation. No need for us to come here again.'

He drew on his cigarette as he summarized: 'So they're heading for Canada.'

'What do we do now, boss?'

'You got some Mandan stock in you. You're a better tracker than I am. You follow those tracks. I'll get back to headquarters and tell 'em what we've found.'

Tyler Morse whacked the ribbons repeatedly on the back of the horses. He gulped air into his lungs in exhilaration. It was cold air, bitingly cold, but it was coming down from Canada. And Canada meant freedom – and a life of luxury.

He was prepared for the worst of the weather that the so-called 'Angel of the Plains' could throw at him. The thick blankets and buffalo-hides that they had purchased from the Lakota were still in the wagon.

Not that the cold meant anything to him.

He had an inner warmth, a warmth that came from self-satisfaction. He'd fooled everybody. From the moment he had set eyes on the yellow metal back in Beauville, his brain had worked overtime. By anybody's calculations a hundred per cent split was better than a fifth. Step by step he had wiped out the participators. And he had a plan, but he had lacked the expertise to follow it through.

Then he'd spotted the blacksmith in Gage City; but from the off he could see the bozo was a home-loving guy. Tyler had seen the type all over the West. Stuck for a dollar, maybe, but the kind to muddle through at the breadline, endlessly optimistic. He'd needed a prod. And Tyler had given him a prod, right in the ass. OK, the guy's woman had died as a result. That was unfortunate maybe; but as someone had once said, you can't make an omelette without breaking eggs.

So he had tricked the blacksmith into coming on board. The poor bozo thought he was onto something good. The sucker. It had just been a matter of disposing of him when he had exceeded his usefulness. The Fayette girl could have been a problem; but she too was now out of the way. He never thought Copperhead would have what it takes to get back into the frame. So, the crazy guy had turned up at the last minute. But like the others he was dead meat now.

Marshal Fullerton clumped into the telegraph office at Fargo. 'Get a cable off to Bismarck pronto.'

The operator grabbed his pencil and pad.

'Beauville gold-heist,' the marshal dictated. 'Wagon with gold known to have been at the old ghost town out at Hard Rock. Tracks headed north.'

He sat down and watched the operative tap out the message. Then he lit a smoke and waited impatiently for a reply. Three cigarettes on, he was sitting at the desk with a piece of paper in his hand.

ONLY REPORTS THAT HAVE COME IN ARE OF KNOWN BUFFALO HUNTERS MOVING WEST, it said. NO REPORTS OF ANY MOVEMENTS NORTH. NOTHING EXCEPT A SMALL WAGON LOADED WITH CHURCH STATUES AND DRIVEN BY PRIESTS.

'Shoot,' he snorted. He crumpled up the missive in frustration and was about to toss it into the waste-basket when he stopped. He flattened it out on the table and stared at the wording once more. 'That's it!' he exclaimed. 'The friggers have melted it down into religious statues!'

He stubbed out his cigarette, leapt to his feet and crossed to the operator. 'Urgent wire to Bismarck...' He stopped. 'No, more important. First a message to Grand Forks law office. If these so-called priests maintain their present course they'll be heading into the jurisdiction of the Grand Forks marshal. So take this down...'

The first thing of which Beatrice became

aware was a tremendous pain in her jaw and cheekbone. With her eyes closed she raised her hand and felt the side of her face. There was a lump on her cheekbone, throbbing and sore.

As she opened her eyes, events came flooding back. She turned to see the still blacksmith lying beside her.

'Gentry!' She rose enough to kneel beside him. His forehead was gashed and blooded. 'Oh, Gentry.' She put her fingers to his nostrils and lips. Could she detect breath? She opened his coat. On the left side his shirt was red. She leant over, put her ear to his chest. There was a beat!

Water, she thought. Where's the pump that Gentry used? She hauled herself to her feet, but then saw the still form of Copperhead further along the street. On her way to the pump, she checked him. But there was no doubt he was dead.

Minutes later she was at Gentry's side. As she dabbed the wet handkerchief around the wound on his brow, his eyelids began to flicker. Although the first thing he saw was Beatrice's face, the first thing that came from his lips was, 'Where is he?'

'Don't mind yourself of him,' she whispered. 'It's you we have to be concerned with now.'

He struggled to rise but fell back with a grunt.

'You've been hit in the side,' she explained.

'I've gotta get him.'

'You're in no condition to get anybody. Don't you remember? You've been shot.'

He tried to look down. 'How bad is it?'

'Don't know till I've had a look at it,' she said. 'But I don't want to open your shirt out here in this cold.'

She helped him to his feet and pulled the arm on his good side round her shoulder. 'Lean on me.'

'You can't take my weight.'

'We don't know until we've tried, do we?'

Slowly she manoeuvred him into the farmhouse and eased him onto the makeshift bed.

‘There’s a lot of blood,’ she said after an examination, ‘but I guess, when I’ve wiped it away, we’ll find it’s not so bad. We can hope, anyway.’

Minutes later her expectations were confirmed. ‘A surface wound. No bullet to probe for, thank goodness. It’s seared you at the waist. When I’ve bandaged it, it should be all right until we can get you to a doctor.’

‘Where you gonna get bandages?’

‘Either out of the goodness of his heart – or more likely to reduce his encumbrances – friend Tyler left my horse and mule. I haven’t got bandages but I’ve got a dress in there somewhere that I can rip up.’

Amongst the load on her mule she also had the makings for refreshment and insisted that Gentry rest and take a drink before he put his mind to anything else. She relit the stove.

His wound strapped but his head still throbbing from the clout of Tyler’s rifle, he sipped at the single tin mug of coffee that they shared in turn. Eventually, despite her protestations, he rose and went outside. Shortly he staggered back in, carrying a rifle and sixgun.

'Poor Copperhead won't have need of these anymore,' he said, 'but I can certainly put them to good use.'

She didn't have to ask his intention. 'You're crazy,' she said. 'You're no gunman.'

He studied the pistol before shoving it into his belt. 'Yeah, I never did get round to practising with this thing.' He laid the rifle down and, looking down at his hands, which he had extended towards the fire, said, 'But these are strong enough to strangle the life out of the rat if I get close.'

'And you're not fit to go chasing across the plains on horseback. Weather's turning harsher too.'

'He killed my Marybelle and I'm gonna kill him.'

She had no answer to that. 'I know I can't stop you – but please take care.' She ran to him and threw her arms round his neck.

'Come back safe – to me.'

He bent his head and kissed the top of her hair. But it was an instinctive action. His mind was elsewhere.

Outside she helped him into the saddle of her horse. Then, slowly, grimacing with pain, he rode to the end of the street looking for tracks that led north. Finding none he went to the other end, eventually seeing recently bent grass. He looked back at Beatrice. She raised her arm, with her other hand apprehensively on her mouth. He tried to return her wave but searing pain prevented him raising his arm. He merely slumped forward in the saddle and clumsily steered his horse in the wake of the man he hated.

FIFTEEN

The plains were savage and unforgiving. But he was oblivious to the cold and wind. He had only one thought. And, despite his wound, the pounding in his head, his lack of expertise with guns, he knew he had advantages. Tyler was leaving clear signs of his passage. Gentry could see the wagon tracks were fresh. Plus, he was no experienced horseback rider but he was following a slower-moving wagon.

He took no cognisance of the honking above as Canada geese flew south. Likewise the buffalo paid him no heed as he passed.

As the hours wore on he slumped further in the saddle. Progressively weaker, he had no thought for himself. No worries that his stamina might not hold out for him to return. His only concern was that he could last out to pay Tyler his deserts.

Suddenly the horse beneath him juddered as its hoof hit a hole. With his hands and legs slack, the unexpected jerking was enough to pitch the weary rider to the ground. He lay there, trying to summon up the strength to rise. Then, the thought of Tyler's wagon wheels still rolling dredged some energy from somewhere and he hauled himself back into the saddle.

Zombielike, he maintained his slow progress, occasionally looking at the ground to ensure he was on the right course. As he lurched in the saddle, it never entered his head that he was probably too weak and inexperienced with a gun to handle Tyler should he ever catch up with him.

Eventually the tracks cut a rutted trail. He paused and studied the ground. Whatever tracks Tyler's wagon had made were now lost amongst the ruts of the existing path. No problem. He knew the man would be heading north. With one glance at the sun to get orientation, he nudged his horse northwards.

Being on an established trail meant the wagon would be able to travel faster. But so could Gentry and he encouraged his horse to a greater pace. But the animal was tiring too and soon slowed down.

The ground was climbing to a low ridge when he heard the faint crackle of rifle fire. He'd been in northern Dakota long enough for the sound to have taken on some familiarity as buffalo hunters plied their grisly trade. But as he neared the rise and the sound became more distinct, he realized this was different. Amidst the thunder of large-bore arms, there was the lighter sound of pistol fire.

Topping the ridge he reined in. In the distance, from the side of the wagon Tyler was battling it out with two figures. Who were they? It couldn't be any of the gang members; they were all dead. It had to be the law. The varmint had been waylaid by the law! For some reason his disguise had ceased to work and in his single-minded madness he had taken them on.

Gentry fell from the saddle and led the horse to the cover of cottonwoods on the ridge to study the tableau. Tyler was by the side of the wagon returning fire with his rifle. The lawmen were at a disadvantage being in exposed positions on the plain, but they were reducing themselves as targets by lying low.

Gentry's only thought was to join in. He wanted some of this. But as he stretched to grab the pommel an excruciating pain again ripped through his side and he fell against the horse. As he paused to gather strength for another attempt he saw one of the lawmen reach a depression and use it as cover to lope around to the other side of the wagon.

Tyler's head pivoted as he scanned the terrain looking for the missing man. But he located him too late. The lawman fired and winged the desperado.

Tyler staggered, then, in his craziness, advanced towards the now exposed officer, jacking in loads and blasting. But they were desperate, haphazard shots. One shot from the lawman was enough to stop his advance, the next grounded him.

Gentry staggered to the tree for firmer support and watched developments. Firing had stopped and Tyler was unmoving on the ground. All Gentry wanted to know was – was the bastard dead?

Keeping their guns levelled, the officers approached carefully and inspected the fallen man. Could be merely wounded, Gentry thought. A man could survive three shots. Knowing Tyler it could be a trick.

The men stood huddled together, exchanging words. Then they sheathed their weapons, bent down and each took one end of the figure.

However, by the way they carelessly swung the shape to one side and then the other in order to use the impetus to dump it over the side into the wagon, Gentry knew the thing they were throwing was lifeless. Tyler was dead.

He hauled himself once more into the

saddle and, slumped forward over the pommel, began the long journey back.

He had been denied the satisfaction of doing it himself.

But an account had been paid.

It was dark when he got back to the derelict farmhouse. The glow of the fire coming from the building was a welcome sight. Equally welcoming was the reception he got from Beatrice, who clung to him in the open doorway, tears in her eyes.

Inside he collapsed onto one of the mattresses.

After he had related the events she made coffee and sat beside him, stroking his hair.

'I'm gonna miss those horses,' he murmured. 'But can't go claiming 'em without getting implicated. They were hard and faithful workers. But I figure they'll be in good hands.'

'And how are you feeling?' she asked, lying beside him.

'At least the headache's gone,' he said,

eyes closed.

'Next thing, young man, is to get you to a doctor in Fargo.'

There was silence as his breathing took on the pattern of sleep.

'What a day,' he murmured. Then, even more faintly: 'And at the end of it – no gold.'

'But what is gold?' she said. 'A shining, transient trouble.'

'Huh?'

'Just something a poet once said.'

'Well, he got that right,' he whispered almost inaudibly. And then he was asleep.

It must have been mid-morning when they finally awoke, after a night huddled in each other's arms. The sleep had had a rejuvenating effect on Gentry; his physical capabilities and mental faculties were coming back to par.

After they had breakfasted they buried Copperhead at the edge of town. The better of the two with words, Beatrice had quoted something appropriate.

The sun had a brightness which had dispelled the cold of the previous night. Gentry took her by the hand and they walked some hundred yards from the buildings. He put his good arm around her and they looked at the flat plains stretching to the horizon.

Canada geese honked overhead. This time he noticed them, and looked up at the massed V-formations.

'Heading south,' he said. 'Boy, have they got the right idea.'

'There's a beauty in this land,' she said, 'but it is of a savage kind. Last night it must have been well below zero. This morning, it could be New England. Or even fair Dixieland in spring.'

'Talking of Dixieland,' he said, 'I been thinking. I know Confederate currency is no longer legal tender but there must be thousands of honest folk in the South still holding it. The new federal government has to do right by them and honour it.'

She looked at him, her expression saying: so what?

'Confederate money must be redeemable by the authorities,' he continued.

'I still don't understand.'

'Back where the gold was hidden, there was a hoard of old Confederate bills. With the prospect of gold bullion, nobody in the caper has paid it the slightest notice. It's there for the taking.'

'No,' she said, 'it won't be there. The lawmen will have located it by now. It's inevitable. The fact that some law agency telegraphed ahead for the officers up north to stop Morse means that they know pretty well the whole story. They'll know about the forge that you used in the ghost town. Before we left, none of us saw any reason to fill in the hole. By now, the lawmen will have searched and found it.'

'Yeah, that's all possible, I agree. Probable even. But there's *also* a chance it *hasn't* been discovered.'

She snuggled closely to him, not caring about gold or Confederate bills or anything else other than the comforting warmth of the man beside her.

'I will let you pursue your flight of fancy, Mr Jones,' she murmured.

'Now, we're going back that way. It won't be much of a detour to drop by the ghost town and see if the bills are still there. If we're in luck we take it. Your mule's a strong fellow, he can handle the extra load. It's only bundles of paper, not like gold.'

He thought on it some more and continued: 'So, when we've picked it up and finally got back south, all we have to do is get an innocent-looking suitcase. We fill it with some of those Confederate bills and cover the whole thing with grime and cobwebs. Then, you go to the monetary agency and spin them a tale, something like you found it in your grandma's attic. That you managed to salvage it from your folks' place before it was burned down. You being a Southern gentlelady, I think you could get away with it.'

Seeing the logic, she nodded.

'We wouldn't try to offload too much in

one go, of course,' he went on, 'because that would arouse suspicion. We'd have to eke it out one batch at a time.'

'Huh,' she smiled. 'You sound like you've learned something from your recent erring from the straight and narrow.'

He ignored the comment and went on. 'So, we wouldn't be coming out of this caper with a fortune like we had the shiny yellow stuff as we intended. But we'd have enough for us to start a new life – together.'

She stepped back and eyed him. 'Gentry Jones, is this a proposal?'

He hesitated, not knowing her reaction. 'Yes, I suppose it is.'

'Mmm,' she mused.

Then a more assertive tone entered her voice: 'Well, we Southern gentleladies like things to be done with proper decorum, young man. So get down on one knee.'

Up above, the geese honked. As though chorusing their approval.

The publishers hope that this book has given you enjoyable reading. Large Print Books are especially designed to be as easy to see and hold as possible. If you wish a complete list of our books please ask at your local library or write directly to:

Dales Large Print Books
Magna House, Long Preston,
Skipton, North Yorkshire.
BD23 4ND

This Large Print Book, for people
who cannot read normal print,
is published under the auspices of
THE ULVERSCROFT FOUNDATION

... we hope you have enjoyed this book.
Please think for a moment about those
who have worse eyesight than you ...
and are unable to even read or enjoy
Large Print without great difficulty.

You can help them by sending a
donation, large or small, to:

The Ulverscroft Foundation,
1, The Green, Bradgate Road,
Anstey, Leicestershire, LE7 7FU,
England.
or request a copy of our brochure for
more details.

The Foundation will use all donations
to assist those people who are visually
impaired and need special attention
with medical research, diagnosis
and treatment.

Thank you very much for your help.